KT-179-593

NEW PENGUIN SHAKESPEARE

GENERAL EDITOR: T. J. B. SPENCER
ASSOCIATE EDITOR: STANLEY WELLS

All's Well That Ends Well Barbara Everett
Antony and Cleopatra Emrys Jones
As You Like It H. J. Oliver
The Comedy of Errors Stanley Wells
Coriolanus G. R. Hibbard
Hamlet T. J. B. Spencer
Henry IV, Part 1 P. H. Davison
Henry IV, Part 2 P. H. Davison
Henry V A. R. Humphreys
Henry VI, Part 1 Norman Sanders
Henry VI, Part 2 Norman Sanders
Henry VI, Part 3 Norman Sanders
Henry VIII A. R. Humphreys
Julius Caesar Norman Sanders
King John R. L. Smallwood
King Lear G. K. Hunter
Love's Labour's Lost John Kerrigan
Macbeth G. K. Hunter
Measure for Measure J. M. Nosworthy
The Merchant of Venice W. Moelwyn Merchant
The Merry Wives of Windsor G. R. Hibbard
A Midsummer Night's Dream Stanley Wells
Much Ado About Nothing R. A. Foakes
The Narrative Poems Maurice Evans
Othello Kenneth Muir
Pericles Philip Edwards
Richard II Stanley Wells
Richard III E. A. J. Honigmann
Romeo and Juliet T. J. B. Spencer
The Sonnets and *A Lover's Complaint* John Kerrigan
The Taming of the Shrew G. R. Hibbard
The Tempest Anne Righter (Anne Barton)
Timon of Athens G. R. Hibbard
Troilus and Cressida R. A. Foakes
Twelfth Night M. M. Mahood
The Two Gentlemen of Verona Norman Sanders
The Two Noble Kinsmen N. W. Bawcutt
The Winter's Tale Ernest Schanzer

WILLIAM SHAKESPEARE

*

KING RICHARD
THE THIRD

EDITED BY
E. A. J. HONIGMANN

PENGUIN BOOKS

230 678

PENGUIN BOOKS

Published by the Penguin Group
Penguin Books Ltd, 27 Wrights Lane, London W8 5TZ, England
Penguin Books USA Inc., 375 Hudson Street, New York, New York 10014, USA
Penguin Books Australia Ltd, Ringwood, Victoria, Australia
Penguin Books Canada Ltd, 10 Alcorn Avenue, Toronto, Ontario, Canada M4V 3B2
Penguin Books (NZ) Ltd, 182–190 Wairau Road, Auckland 10, New Zealand

Penguin Books Ltd, Registered Offices: Harmondsworth, Middlesex, England

This edition first published in Penguin Books 1968
20

This edition copyright © Penguin Books, 1968
Introduction and Notes copyright © E. A. J. Honigmann, 1968
All rights reserved

Printed in England by Clays Ltd, St Ives plc
Set in Monotype Ehrhardt

Except in the United States of America, this book is sold subject
to the condition that it shall not, by way of trade or otherwise, be lent,
re-sold, hired out, or otherwise circulated without the publisher's
prior consent in any form of binding or cover other than that in
which it is published and without a similar condition including this
condition being imposed on the subsequent purchaser

CONTENTS

INTRODUCTION 7

FURTHER READING 47

KING RICHARD THE THIRD 51

COMMENTARY 201

AN ACCOUNT OF THE TEXT 242

GENEALOGICAL TABLES 255

NORWICH CITY COLLEGE LIBRARY

Stock No.	230678		
Class	822.33 K RIC 3		
Cat.	SSA	Proc.	3UL

INTRODUCTION

THE popularity of *Richard III* dates back to Shakespeare's own lifetime. Six editions of the play were published between 1597 and 1622 in Quarto, to be followed by a seventh in the Folio of 1623; and the exceptional number of early editions is matched by the exceptional number of copies of these editions still known to exist. Early allusions to the play confirm that it probably ranked with *Romeo and Juliet* and *Hamlet* as one of the outstanding favourites of the theatre; indeed, *Richard III* seems to have been one of the first plays to feature in the 'Shakespeare mythos', as we learn from the Diary of John Manningham, a student at the Middle Temple, in the year 1602.

> *Upon a time when Burbage played Richard III there was a [female] citizen grew so far in liking with him, that before she went from the play she appointed him to come that night unto her by the name of Richard III. Shakespeare, overhearing their conclusion, went before, was entertained and at his game ere Burbage came. The message being brought that Richard III was at the door, Shakespeare caused return to be made that William the Conqueror was before Richard III.*

Whether or not the story is true – witty anecdotes readily attach themselves to the famous – it does at least establish that by 1602 the play had become part of popular mythology.

Any account of the glamour and power of *Richard III* must, of course, begin with Richard himself. The play's

7

vitality depends upon its central character more completely than that of any other work of Shakespeare – so much so that '*Richard III* without Richard' seems more unthinkable than '*Hamlet* without the prince'. Yet Richard, a subtler psychological study than any previously exhibited in an English theatre, cannot be said to have been created, but only to have been touched up and improved, by Shakespeare, who drew upon several different sources of inspiration.

In the English chronicles of Edward Hall (1548) and Raphael Holinshed (1577, 1587) Shakespeare had the good fortune to find a portrait of his hero that was already a finished work of art. The chronicles provided a general assessment of character, and presented suggestive psychological details in a narrative that switches every so often into direct speech and all the tensions of drama. Without some idea of the quality of this historical literature one cannot appreciate the distinctive excellence of Shakespeare's play, and I therefore quote some extracts (from the second edition of Holinshed, volume 3). First, Richard's appearance, character, and general behaviour.

> *Richard, the third son ... was in wit and courage equal with either of them [his brothers], in body and prowess far under them both, little of stature, ill-featured of limbs, crook-backed, his left shoulder much higher than his right, hard favoured of visage. ... He was malicious, wrathful, envious, and from afore his birth ever froward. It is for truth reported that the Duchess his mother had so much ado in her travail, that she could not be delivered of him uncut; and that he came into the world with the feet forward ... and, as the fame runneth also, not untoothed.*
>
> (p. 712; compare II.4.27–9, IV.4.163–8)

*When he stood musing, he would bite and chew busily his
nether lip; as who said that his fierce nature in his cruel
body always chafed, stirred, and was ever unquiet: beside
that, the dagger which he wore he would, when he studied,
with his hand pluck up and down in the sheath to the midst,
never drawing it fully out: he was of a ready, pregnant, and
quick wit, wily to feign, and apt to dissemble.*

(p. 760; compare IV.2.27)

Richard's malice, wrath, envy, dissimulation, and wit all
received special attention in the dramatic portrait, as also
his restlessness, concerning which Shakespeare may have
given private instructions to his principal actor. It is an
interesting fact that Samuel Rowlands in *The Letting of
Humour's Blood* (1600) said of 'gallants' that they

> ... *like Richard the usurper, swagger,
> That had his hand continual on his dagger*

– for, since Rowlands went on to ask 'Or shall we to the
Globe and see a play?', it seems that Richard's characteristic touch was observed in Shakespeare's *Richard III*.
Shakespeare could have mentioned it personally to Bur-
bage, since the text of the play as it survives fails to do so –
though we learn in passing that Richard wore a dagger
(III.1.110).

A list of Richard's general qualities provided Shakespeare
with a useful starting-point. The vivid detail and dramatic
scene-building of the chronicles gave him something infi-
nitely more valuable – an understanding of state affairs and
of human deviousness quite beyond his earlier range. For
the best of these scenes both he and Holinshed and Hall
were indebted to Sir Thomas More. The words, as we
now know them, are Shakespeare's, but the penetrating
intelligence is often More's. As an illustration I cite from

More's account of the fall of Hastings, as transmitted by Holinshed, adding some cross-references to the play.

We hear that Richard and Buckingham sent Catesby 'to prove with some words cast out afar off' whether Hastings would side with them (compare III.1.170), and learnt that he could not be moved. Discussing the 'two several Councils' with Derby, Hastings expressed his confidence in Catesby who, he thought, would inform him of all that went on (III.2.12–24). The night before Hastings' death Derby had his prophetic dream that 'a boar with his tusks ... razed them both by the heads' (III.2.11), and sent a 'trusty messenger' to his friend to suggest flight (III.2.1), only to provoke Hastings' mockery. In the morning a knight called on Hastings, ostensibly out of politeness but in fact to hasten him to his doom at the Tower. When Hastings stopped on his way to chat to a priest the knight 'said merrily ... "What, my lord, I pray you come on, whereto talk you so long with that priest? You have no need of a priest yet": and therewith he laughed upon him, as though he would say, "Ye shall have soon"' (III.2.107). Proceeding to the Tower, Hastings met 'one Hastings, a pursuivant of his own name', whom he had previously encountered while being led to prison, and he hints that his former enemies are about to be beheaded at Pomfret (III.2.94 ff.) – which was devised by Richard to happen 'about the self same hour' as Hastings' own execution (III.3).

The great scene in the Tower (III.4) starts with Richard's late arrival, 'excusing himself that he had been from them so long; saying merrily that he had been a sleeper that day'.

After a little talking with them, he said unto the Bishop of Ely: 'My lord, you have very good strawberries at your garden in Holborn, I require you to let us have a mess of them.' 'Gladly, my lord,' quoth he, 'would God I had some better thing as ready to your pleasure as that!' And therewithal in all the haste he sent his servant for a mess of strawberries. The Protector . . . thereupon, praying them to spare him for a little while, departed thence. And soon after one hour, between ten and eleven, he returned into the chamber amongst them all, changed, with a wonderful sour, angry countenance, knitting the brows, frowning and fretting, and gnawing on his lips. . . .

Then, when he had sitten still a while, thus he began: 'What were they worthy to have that compass and imagine the destruction of me, being so near of blood unto the King, and Protector of his royal person and his realm?' At this question, all the lords sat sore astonished. . . . Then the Lord Chamberlain [Hastings], as he that for the love between them thought he might be boldest with him, answered and said that they were worthy to be punished as heinous traitors, whatsoever they were. And all the other affirmed the same. 'That is,' quoth he, 'yonder sorceress my brother's wife, and other with her,' meaning the Queen. . . .

Then said the Protector: 'Ye shall all see in what wise that sorceress, and that other witch of her counsel, Shore's wife, with their affinity, have, by their sorcery and witchcraft, wasted my body.' And therewith he plucked up his doublet sleeve to his elbow, upon his left arm, where he showed a weerish [shrivelled] withered arm, and small; as it was never other.

Hereupon every man's mind sore misgave them, well perceiving that this matter was but a quarrel. . . . Nevertheless, the Lord Chamberlain, which from the death of King Edward kept Shore's wife . . . answered and said: 'Certainly, my lord, if they have so heinously done, they be worthy heinous punishment.'

'What!' quoth the Protector, 'thou servest me, I ween,

*with " ifs" and with " ands" ! I tell thee they have so done,
and that I will make good on thy body, traitor !' And therewith, as in a great anger, he clapped his fist upon the board
a great rap. At which token one cried 'Treason!'
without the chamber. Therewith a door clapped, and in
come there rushing men in harness, as many as the chamber
might hold. And anon the Protector said to the Lord
Hastings: 'I arrest thee, traitor !' 'What me, my lord?'
quoth he. 'Yes, thee, traitor !' quoth the Protector. . . .*

*Then were they all quickly bestowed in diverse chambers,
except the Lord Chamberlain, whom the Protector bade
speed and shrive him apace, 'for, by Saint Paul !' quoth
he, 'I will not to dinner till I see thy head off !' It booted
him not to ask why, but heavily he took a priest at adven-
ture, and made a short shrift : for a longer would not be
suffered, the Protector made so much haste to dinner,
which he might not go to, until this were done, for saving of
his oath* (pages 722–3).

Shortened, these scenes lose some of their power. Yet
even in a single extract Sir Thomas More's ironic and
dramatic genius astounds. For Shakespeare it was a wonderful stroke of luck to stumble, in Holinshed or Hall,
upon a mind, one of the very few, that could enlarge his
own: and the difference between his pedestrian three-part
Henry VI and his vibrantly artistic *Richard III* is a measure
of what he learnt. The whole of the third Act leans heavily
upon More, the Buckingham scenes (5—7) no less than
those about Hastings: and, though there are other reasons
as well (see p. 29), it may be that Richard's psychological
change in IV.4 fails to carry complete conviction partly
because Shakespeare's tutor broke off writing at just this
point, abandoning him to lesser men.

Let us glance quickly at the other historical literature

that lies behind *Richard III*. The story, as Shakespeare read it in Hall and Holinshed, traces back to two early sixteenth-century accounts, More's life of Richard (Latin and English) and Polydore Vergil's *Anglica Historia*, neither of which he himself seems to have looked at. Later chronicles borrowed freely from these two near-contemporary historians, and from each other, in the usual manner of the time. Richard Grafton (1543) used both, and was himself plundered by Hall (1548), from whom Grafton then extracted more bits and pieces for his second version (1569). Holinshed, finally, drew upon More, Polydore Vergil, Hall, Grafton, and others. These texts are often so close, reprinting a page or more word for word, that we cannot always say with certainty that one rather than another was consulted; though Shakespeare glanced at a second chronicle for facts not mentioned by Holinshed, and I have called it Hall's, it could just as well have been Grafton's (1569).

Apart from using two prose chronicles for general information Shakespeare must have been indebted for minor points to various plays and poems. In *A Mirror for Magistrates* (1559, 1563, etc.), where the ghosts of several of the leading persons of the play bewail their misfortunes, that of Clarence accuses his murderers, who

> ... *in a butt of malmsey standing by*
> *New christened me, because I should not cry.*

From Holinshed Shakespeare only learnt that Clarence 'was cast into the Tower, and therewith adjudged for a traitor, and privily drowned in a butt of malmsey' (p. 703: compare I.4.157, 273). Unable to resist the jest about 'new christening', he assigned it to Richard (I.1.49–50); and a few other details come from *A Mirror* as well.

The relationship of Shakespeare's *Richard III* to the

anonymous *True Tragedy of Richard III* (1594) raises more
elusive questions. At least one of these two plays borrowed
extensively from the other, for *True Tragedy* covers much
the same ground as *Richard III* – the reconciliation of the
nobles and death of King Edward, the fall of the Queen's
kindred and the Queen's taking of sanctuary, the fall of
Hastings, the murder of the princes, the fall of Buckingham, Derby's double-dealing with Richard, Bosworth –
with some notable minor differences, such as the promin-
ence given to Shore's wife, a lady excluded from Shakespeare's play in person, if not as a topic of conversation
(I.1.73, 93, III.1.185, etc.). At the other end of the scale
there are striking echoes, in particular Richard's cry at
Bosworth, 'A horse! A horse! My kingdom for a horse!'
(V.4.7) and 'A horse, a horse, a fresh horse!' (*True Tragedy*).

Unfortunately *True Tragedy* survives only in a corrupt
text, and the many verbal and episodic resemblances of
the two plays may therefore be variously explained. There
must have been a textually sound *True Tragedy* (hereafter
True Tragedy i), which may have ante-dated *Richard III*
and influenced Shakespeare; or *True Tragedy i* could have
followed *Richard III*, and been inspired by it. Whichever
of these two views we adopt, it is likely that *True Tragedy ii*,
the text of 1594, conflates and garbles both *True Tragedy i*
and Shakespeare's *Richard III*.

If only we knew when Shakespeare wrote *Richard III*,
the relationship of the two dramatic versions might be
settled. But we cannot pretend to know, we merely guess.
Some experts date Shakespeare's play as early as 1588–9,
others as late as 1593–4. Should the latter be correct one
could then happily debate, among other things, the con-
nexion between *Richard III* and both Giles Fletcher's
poem, *The Rising to the Crown of Richard III* (1593), and
Anthony Chute's poem, *Shore's Wife* (1593). But it is

time to end such unprofitable speculation, and I shall simply state my preference. I believe that *Richard III* dates from the latter part of Shakespeare's 'first period', and probably preceded the authorized (lost) version of *True Tragedy* (*True Tragedy i*): accordingly, and also because it seems unwise to base discussion of Shakespeare's 'source' on a text as corrupt as *True Tragedy ii*, I refer chiefly to Holinshed and Hall.

No praise is too high for the psychological and political acuteness of the chronicle sources, but of their historical impartiality one cannot speak so well. They all subscribe *manibus et pedibus* to the myth of a fiend-like king. To account for the acuteness and the prejudice we have only to remember that the story traces back to Sir Thomas More, who served in his youth in the household of Cardinal Morton, formerly Bishop of Ely – a leading opponent of Richard, first seen in the play as a pawn, fit to be sent on errands (III.4.31), but later recognized as a formidable chess-piece that may mate a king (IV.3.49–50). From Morton and other senior survivors Sir Thomas More inherited the prejudice that was accentuated by succeeding chroniclers, who no doubt blackened Richard to gratify their Tudor sovereigns.

Modern historians paint a very different picture: they find no fault in Richard's early years, admit that he had his constructive side as a ruler, and regard the murder of Hastings as the fatal error of judgement that led to all that followed. Some have even tried to prove Richard not guilty of the death of the two princes in the Tower; but the majority still holds with the common opinion of the time that the chief beneficiary had the greatest motive. Be that as it may, both Richard's moral and his physical deformity were for long exaggerated. Of the latter Professor C. L. Kingsford wrote: 'Tradition represents Richard as deformed. It seems clear that he had some physical defect, though not so great as has been alleged. Extant portraits show an intellectual face characteristic of the early Renaissance, but do not indicate any deformity' (*Encyclopaedia Britannica*, 1956 edition).

Shakespeare firmly identified Richard in Act I as a fiend, a cacodemon, and stressed his hunchback, his limp (I.1.23), his withered arm (III.4.68). In the very act of finalizing the Tudor myth the dramatist seems, nevertheless, to have had his doubts. He meditated about historical distortion (II.4.27–34), a subject that worried him, for he returned to it – so that one wonders whether he divined instinctively that the chronicles misrepresented Richard, and asked *himself*, 'Is it upon record, or else reported?' (III.1.72).

At the same time, though anxious to preserve the psychological facts of the story, he had to give it a dramatic shape, and in order to do this felt compelled to adjust historical details. Close as he sometimes comes to the characterization, scene-building, and very words of Holinshed, particularly in Act III, he can also switch over to grossly telescoped history, as in IV.4.433–538. Here he crammed together various risings against Richard of the year 1483 (Buckingham, Richmond's first fruitless voyage to England, Courtney, the Guildfords) and the events of 1485 (Richmond's second voyage and landing at Milford Haven). So too, all four scenes of the first Act, where Shakespeare invents much more freely than in the rest of the play, are expanded from a few scattered sentences in the chronicles: the removal of King Henry's body from St Paul's soon after his death (1471); the wooing of Anne (1472); the murder of Clarence (1478). One should not react too censoriously to such faking, for what, after all, does it matter if events are slightly reshuffled? Shakespeare never mentions dates, and manifestly took very little interest in them.

Before leaving the chronicles we must observe that Shakespeare sometimes nodded, accepting a strange speech or action from the sources and forgetting to transfer the motive, as when Richard and Buckingham enter 'in rotten armour, marvellous ill-favoured' (III.5.0). Holinshed can clarify this:

> [*Richard*] *with the Duke of Buckingham stood harnessed in old ill faring briganders [armour], such as no man should ween that they would vouchsafe to have put upon their backs except that some sudden necessity had constrained them* (p. 724).

Buckingham's tactlessness, when he reports to Richard (III.7.12–14) that he told the Londoners that Richard's 'lineaments' are 'the right idea' of his father, 'Both in your form and nobleness of mind', results, again, from an oversight. In the chronicles only Richard's face, not his general form, was compared with his father's: 'in the lineaments and favour of his visage, [Richard] represented the very face of the noble duke his father' (Holinshed, p. 727).

Several times, too, Shakespeare refers to Queen Elizabeth's 'brothers' (I.3.37, III.1.6, etc.), though Rivers is her only brother in the play; it has been plausibly suggested that he supposed Grey, whom he nowhere calls her son, to be her brother. An even stranger misunderstanding lies behind II.1.69, where Lord Woodville and Lord Scales are separately addressed after Lord Rivers, though all three titles belonged to Rivers; evidently Shakespeare read too quickly a passage in Hall, 'this young prince was committed to Lord Anthony Woodville Earl Rivers and Lord Scales', and thought that three persons were meant!

17

Whether or not Shakespeare slipped in supplying no more than hints about the treachery that led to Buckingham's capture is less easy to decide. Abjuring all enmity to the Queen, Buckingham hopes that if he forgets his oath he will be punished in his greatest need by a friend's treachery (II.1.32 ff.), and later recalls that his wish has come true (V.1.13). Buckingham's son states the facts in *Henry VIII* (II.1.107–11): his father, 'Flying for succour to his servant Banister' was 'by that wretch betrayed'. While writing Act II of *Richard III* Shakespeare perhaps planned a later scene depicting the treachery of Banister whom, according to Holinshed, Buckingham 'above all men loved, favoured, and trusted' – a grand climax after the play's other acts of treachery. If so, he changed his mind. I think it possible that the Buckingham scenes were slightly changed before the play was finished: prophecy and fulfilment dovetail so meticulously elsewhere that it is odd that Buckingham has not foretold his death on All Souls' Day, as he asserts several times in V.1. The Folio's omission of the 'clock-passage' (IV.2.98–115) suggests, again, that a Buckingham scene was tampered with; this superb passage could have been an afterthought, though this is no longer the favourite explanation (see pp. 229–30).

*

In Hall and Holinshed Shakespeare's Richard stands before us almost fully formed. Upon the historical portrait a second image was nevertheless superimposed – that of the Machiavel, a type whose importance in the English theatre dates from the arrival in London of Christopher Marlowe (*c.* 1587). Some of the peculiarities of the type were already found in Lorenzo, the villain of Kyd's *Spanish Tragedy* (*c.* 1586), as in some earlier and slighter dramatic sketches. Marlowe, however, understood the detested

Machiavel more profoundly than any predecessor, perhaps because he recognized himself in the part, in Barabas as in Faustus. Love of power and mischief-making, a quick wit, a magnetic personality, the habit of gloating and self-gratulation, prominent features of the Marlovian Machiavel and, apparently, of Marlowe the man, all reappear in Shakespeare's Richard – who already boasts in *3 Henry VI* that he can 'set the murderous Machiavel to school' (III.2.193).

One thinks of the distinctively Marlovian hero as, in the first instance, a superman – the Machiavel being only one of his Marlovian disguises. The cult of the superman also has its bearing on *Richard III*, where Shakespeare attempted his first full-scale study of the type. Like Tamburlaine, Barabas, and the rest, Richard pits himself against society and against the heavens and, for a time, prevails. He delights, like the others, in theatrical gestures and even – a contemporary touch – in degrading forms of sensationalism. For Marlowe and the new Revenge Tragedy, both influenced by the revival of interest in Seneca, had combined to popularize torture-scenes and the sick humour of wittily contrived deaths. These new fashions are reflected in the dialogue of Clarence's murderers (I.4.99 ff.), in the cat-and-mouse game with Hastings (III.2.35–III.4.79), in the masochism of Richard's two wooing-scenes (I.2, IV.4.199 ff.), and elsewhere. The Vice of the old Moralities, a more remote ancestor with whom Richard actually compares himself (III.1.82–3) –

> *Thus, like the formal Vice, Iniquity,*
> *I moralize two meanings in one word*

– was now elevated to a more serious and central position in the new drama of the 1580s, and by none more than by

Marlowe, the champion of individualism against official morality.

Shakespeare's greatest debt to Marlowe was a general intellectual one. In his last years Marlowe (1564–93) waged war against received ideas, both as a dramatist and in his private life: 'almost into every company [into which] he cometh', one acquaintance said, 'he persuades men to atheism'. If we may believe his accusers he urged that religion was a mere plot '*to keep* men *in awe*', and inveighed blasphemously against the Bible and biblical personages. In plays like *Tamburlaine* (*c*. 1587) and *Doctor Faustus* (*c*.1589) he managed to question traditional Christian ideas without aligning himself too inextricably with the disaffected: one cannot imagine that before Marlowe's time public gatherings were titillated in this way, though secret societies had long continued a tradition of anti-Christian thinking. By bringing this tradition into the open Marlowe prepared the way for Richard of Gloucester's mask of sanctimoniousness, and his many blasphemous witticisms ('Else wherefore breathe I in a Christian land?', 'O, do not swear, my lord of Buckingham'), and perhaps Shakespeare acknowledged this when he made Richard echo Marlowe's fundamental position ('Conscience . . . Devised at first *to keep* the strong *in awe*', V.3.310–11).

One recent editor has said that Richard's sanctimoniousness was inspired by nothing more than the brief reference in Hall to the two bishops used as stage-props in the audience with the Lord Mayor (III.7.94 ff.), together with Sir Thomas More's irony about Richard's being 'sent out of heaven into this vicious world for the amendment of men's manners'. This is a strange misinterpretation. Shakespeare's Richard repeatedly invokes God's name – but so does Holinshed's. The one declares 'I thank my God for my humility!' (II.1.74), the other, less succinctly, tells the lords 'for never shall I, by God's grace, so wed myself to mine own will, but that I shall be ready to change it upon your better advices' (Holinshed, p. 717). And if Shakespeare relished and emphasized Richard's hypocritical 'devotion and right Christian zeal' in the scene with the bishops, he drew inspiration from another episode in the same historical series, omitted in the play. Doctor Shaw (mentioned at III.5.102) was prevailed upon by the Protector's party to preach at Paul's Cross, there to allege the bastardy of King Edward's children and Richard's right to the crown. (In the play Buckingham takes over Doctor Shaw's arguments, at III.7.1–19.) It was planned that Richard

> should have comen in among the people to the sermon-ward, to the end that those words meeting with his presence, might have been taken among the hearers, as though the Holy Ghost had put them in the preacher's mouth ... (Holinshed, p. 727).

Not even Shakespeare's Richard was a more impious stage-manager, though he chose better actors than Dr Shaw, who (in the chronicles) bungled his job. Another example of fake piety, where Shakespeare is even closer to his source but seems to me not to have reproduced all of its acid humour, follows Richard's oath not to dine till he has seen Hastings' head (see p. 12). In the play (III.4.76–95) Richard is merely in a great hurry; in Holinshed Hastings must make 'short shrift' since 'the Protector made so much haste to dinner, which he might not go to, until this were done, *for saving of his oath*' (p. 723).

Richard's religious mask was already part of the man in the chronicles, but it is true that the gleefulness of his imposture was added by Shakespeare. The dramatic effectiveness of such glee Shakespeare had learnt from the old Vice and, in more sophisticated form, from Marlowe – and had already essayed with his Aaron the Moor in *Titus Andronicus*. Lesser writers also recognized that Marlowe's vein of blasphemy could be rewarding. As Robert Greene complained in his *Farewell to Folly* (1591), the 'blasphemous rhetoric' of those who 'bring Scripture' into the theatre had got out of hand.

> *As, for example, two lovers on the stage arguing one another of unkindness, his mistress runs over him with this canonical sentence, 'A man's conscience is a thousand witnesses,' and her knight again excuseth himself with that saying of the Apostle, 'Love covereth the multitude of sins.' I think this was but simple abusing of the Scripture.*

That both of the quotations that angered Greene were in Shakespeare's mind as he wrote *Richard III* is a strange coincidence. Richard tells Lady Anne and Queen Elizabeth that the motive for all his sins was love (I.2.114–24, 189; IV.4.288), and exclaims later 'My conscience hath a thousand several tongues' (V.3.194: compare V.2.17). Marlowe's witty profanity had caught on, and *Richard III* evidently owed much to the new cult.

*

Though included among the 'Histories' in the Folio collection of 1623, *Richard III* was previously known as a tragedy. It was entered as such in the Stationers' Register (1597), and both the title-page of the first Quarto (1597) and Francis Meres in the earliest surviving allusion to the play (1598) thus described it. The head-title in the Folio announced 'The Tragedy of Richard the Third', and the dialogue itself, employing more cognates of 'tragedy' than any other Shakespearian play, gives a further clue to the author's attitude (*tragic*, II.2.39; *tragedy*, III.2.59; *tragedian*, III.5.5; *tragical*, IV.4.7). But what sort of tragedy? There can be little doubt that Shakespeare had in mind the medieval idea that a tragedy records the rise and fall of princes, to which he alludes in passing in IV.4.86 – 'One heaved a-high to be hurled down below'. For a less laconic definition we may consult Chaucer's Monk.

> *I wol biwaille, in manere of tragedie,*
> *The harm of hem that stoode in heigh degree*
> *And fillen so that ther nas no remedie ...*
> *For certain, whan that Fortune list to flee*
> *Ther may no man the cours of hire withholde. ...*

While *Richard III* owed much to Marlovian and to Senecan tragedy, the medieval idea gave the play its shape – its two-phase movement. Fortune's wheel (see IV.4.105), which casts down the wicked unexpectedly, turns just as Richard seems to have triumphed, at the beginning of Act IV. The chronicles, as it happens, had already hinted at such a pattern. The murder of the princes was seen not only as a decisive event politically, in so far as it set the country against Richard, but also psychologically.

> *I have heard by credible report of such as were secret with his chamberlain that, after this abominable deed done, he never had a quiet mind. ... Where he went abroad, his eyes whirled about, his body privily fenced, his hand ever upon his dagger ...* (Holinshed, p. 735).

Shakespeare closely linked the murder and coronation (IV.2.3–18), and elaborated the idea of Richard's moral collapse. Before the murder his Richard always holds the initiative, moving so swiftly that he throws all his opponents into confusion; after it he himself is frequently out-manoeuvred. Sometimes an instance of his tactical genius

lay at hand in Holinshed (the fall of Hastings – compare
p. 10), but more often Shakespeare invented or retouched
the facts. It is true that Richard married the Lady Anne,
widow of Edward, Prince of Wales (according to Holinshed's chronicle), but not that he persuaded her from
loathing to love in the presence of her father-in-law's
corpse in the brief time symbolized by less than two
hundred lines of dialogue. Richard's dramatic entrance
and verbal storms in I.3 derive from vague general remarks
about his rivalry with the Queen's kindred; for his effectively timed announcement of Clarence's death (II.1.81)
Shakespeare alone was responsible; and, though Holinshed
mentioned (p. 712) that some suspected that Richard
'lacked not in helping forth his brother of Clarence to his
death', he, like modern historians, evidently thought the
Queen's party to blame (p. 703), whereas Shakespeare
made the murder one of Richard's many premeditated
moves towards the crown.

Already in *3 Henry VI*, as Richard's character took firm
shape in Shakespeare's mind, we hear that 'He's sudden,
if a thing comes in his head' (V.5.86). Just as his 'sudden-
ness' begins to overreach itself (*Richard III*, IV.2) he frets,
significantly, that others are too slow (IV.2.18–20) –

> *Shall I be plain? I wish the bastards dead,*
> *And I would have it suddenly performed.*
> *What sayst thou now? Speak suddenly, be brief.*

Then his instantaneous decision to drop the man who made
him king, as Buckingham hesitates about the murder of the
princes, is entirely unhistorical. In Holinshed the two
allies quarrel because Buckingham demanded the Earl of
Hereford's lands (p. 736), previously offered by Richard
as the reward for his support (p. 721: compare III.1.194 ff.);
after his coronation Richard discovered that the lands in

question were 'somewhat interlaced with the title to the crown', and consequently

> *rejected the Duke's request with many spiteful and minatory words. Which so wounded his heart with hatred and mistrust, that he never after could endure to look aright on King Richard, but ever feared his own life* (p. 736).

Buckingham himself is quoted complaining of Richard's 'taunts and retaunts' (p. 739), and he goes on to condemn the murder of the princes, 'to the which, God be my judge, I never agreed'. Shakespeare switched the two issues round: he made the murder of the two princes the all-important one and, suppressing the point that the Hereford lands were 'interlaced' with the crown, reduced them to a mere pretext for a quarrel. Since the interests of the two men do not clash, Richard pounces on his victim the more unexpectedly.

After the murder of the princes Richard himself is taken by surprise again and again, and his brilliant control of events, and, ultimately, his self-control, deserts him. True, the first news of the counter-movement precedes the murder, and Richard continues to exercise some initiative. But the cumulative effect is overpowering as we learn that Richard's active opponents include Richmond (IV.1), Dorset (IV.2), Morton and Buckingham (IV.3), his own mother (IV.4), and Derby (IV.5), as well as rebels in Devonshire, Kent, Yorkshire, and Milford Haven (IV.4). The tactics of surprise now work against him, undermining his confidence: he becomes irritable, antagonizes his friends, panics under pressure, suffers from bad dreams, and awakes in terror. Gleefully aggressive before the murder, grimly defensive after it – the change is complete.

In stage-presentation the fairly crude formal contrast between the two halves of the play must be given full emphasis. Richard breaks in upon others with maximum *éclat* in the first half and at once takes command, even in the royal presence (II.1). Later the tables are turned: he is himself waylaid and, though now king, forced to yield to the commanding personality of his mother (IV.4); messengers burst in upon him, ghosts break in upon his sleep; in the end the unexpected entry of a friend startles him (V.3.209), while his enemies intrude so far as to pin papers on to his tents (V.3.304). Only after perceiving this formal contrast can one appreciate some of the play's more oblique effects. Richard pretends to fear a sudden attack by his enemies ('Look back! Defend thee! Here are enemies!' – III.5.19), and arranges to have himself 'interrupted' while at prayer (III.7.94). Here the surface humour is obvious enough: one has encountered his piety and his fear of secret enemies before. But in so far as he postures as 'a man easily broken in upon' we sense a deeper humour – Richard's ironic self-awareness, his technique.

The formal contrast between the two halves of the play is also sustained by the antithesis of Richard's intellectual vigour and decline. To some extent this contrast is more apparent than real, inasmuch as Richard grapples at first with simple, unequal opponents (Clarence, Hastings, Lady Anne, etc.), who allow him to win easily, while his later ones are more perceptive, and of course have more reason to be so. The few who almost rival Richard in penetration at the beginning (York, Queen Margaret) are powerless, and therefore he need not exert himself when their shafts bounce off him harmlessly. (His wit-combat with York, in particular, gives the impression of a superior mind refusing to engage with a clever but negligible enemy: III.1.102 ff.) Thus his intellectual supremacy seems beyond question. Again, Richard's verbal wit, of which we see less in the second half, becomes less necessary to him once he is on the throne; from that moment he uses blunter instruments, and perhaps justifiably (from his point of view), in which case it would be unfair to talk of a mind in decline.

Though, as I have indicated, Shakespeare may have heightened the contrast deceptively, a real decline does show itself in the second half. The clearest evidence comes in IV.4, when he exposes himself to the snubs of his mother and of Queen Elizabeth. Granted, he has a motive; and he foreknows that he will not be treated kindly. What is significant, however, is the number of times he blunders into verbal traps – in short, his failure to control the conversation. How different from the dexterity of his earlier encounters!

> *You mock me, madam; this is not the way*
> *To win your daughter.*

These words (IV.4.284–5) betray a mind reeling back upon itself and totally unable to dart to the offensive; they lack Richard's earlier resilience. His next speech ('Say that I did all this for love of her') falls back upon the very arguments already employed with Lady Anne (I.2.121 ff.), and thus sounds mechanical, uninspired; when, thereupon, he tries to swear his good faith and Queen Elizabeth repeatedly cuts him off (IV.4.366 ff.) we cannot help recalling the occasion when *he* successfully cut off Queen Margaret (I.3.233); when, finally, he joins the ranks of those who call for retribution against themselves if their professions are insincere (IV.4.397 ff.), he degrades himself to the intellectual level of the other petty intriguers who had earlier failed to foresee the inevitable. These impressions are swiftly confirmed when, in the very next scene, just after Richard thinks he has triumphed, it transpires that the Queen in fact overreached him, and only pretended to consent to her daughter's marriage, presumably to play for time.

The view that the Queen outwitted Richard goes back to the eighteenth century. (Cibber, in his adaptation of the play, added an aside to show that her consent is only a ruse.) But some now think such a reading too heavily ironical at Richard's expense, and prefer Richard's assessment of the Queen as a 'shallow, changing woman' (IV.4.431): she agrees to Richard's proposal, and later to the Richmond marriage. I revert to the older interpretation, for two reasons. First, increasing irony at Richard's expense is built into the structure of the play. Second, though not previously depicted as Richard's match intellectually,* the Queen proves herself precisely that in her quick-witted line-by-line exchanges with him shortly before she agrees – like Derby (see p. 40) she grows more devious as she learns to understand events.

Changes in Richard's speech-habits also signalize his intellectual and moral deterioration. Before Act IV his every insult seems carefully timed: he always loses his patience or temper to advantage (I.3.42, II.1.79, and, notably, III.4.59, III.7.140), and can keep them under direst provocation (III.1.102 ff.). During his *éclaircissement* with Buckingham he first speaks unguardedly, and thenceforth continues to do so (for example, V.3.8, 73–4, 222–3, 309–12). One might label some of these incautious speeches asides, but, contributing as they do to the sense of Richard's growing recklessness, they are best left alone. Richard's broken and irregular lines in V.3.47–79 also help to suggest a disturbed mind, and contrast strikingly with the regularity of Richmond's, expressive of a mind at peace within itself.

On the physical level there is a similar contrast: excep-

* Yet 'deep-revolving' Buckingham thinks her 'subtle' (III.1.152).

tional vigour in the first half, and after it a decline. Contempt for the 'weak piping time of peace' (I.1.24), love of bustle (I.1.152), the many references to Richard's butcheries, as also the animal-images used for him (dog, boar, pack-horse, etc.), all underline his physical exuberance and strength. The fact that he can call a messenger a 'tardy cripple' (II.1.91), though himself a cripple, testifies to his vitality. Just before the end his own words point the other way: 'I will not sup tonight', 'What, is my beaver *easier than it was?*', 'Look that my staves be sound *and not too heavy*' (V.3.48–65). Earlier allusions to his sleeplessness prepared for the change (IV.1.82 ff.: this actually precedes the coronation and murder, but is associated with them in dramatic time; IV.2.72);* and a producer must, I think, indicate growing physical fatigue beneath Richard's nervousness from the fourth Act onwards.

Duplicate scenes also underscore the play's two-phase movement. Clarence's dream and Richard's are intimately connected (I.4, V.3; see p. 34), Queen Margaret's second appearance is deliberately repetitive, the murder of Clarence anticipates that of the princes. Those who deplore a 'loss of inspiration' in Richard's second wooing-scene (IV.4.199 ff.) should therefore ask themselves whether the failure was Shakespeare's or Richard's. If the scene conforms to a larger strategy of duplication and plot-movement Richard's deficiencies must have been planned.

Yet, undeniably, something goes wrong in the play's second half. One perceives an aesthetic reason for the two-phase movement, the rise-and-fall effect, without feeling fully convinced of the identity of the later Richard and his earlier namesake. Despite the brilliance of his portrait, characterization is sacrificed to plot. The very patness of

* Similarly Richard's superstition, when he hears of Rouge-mount (IV.2.102 ff.), falls into the second part of the play in *dramatic* time.

some of the reversals, such as that implied by 'Have mercy, Jesu!' (V.3.179), while contributing to the sense of formal design, simplifies character almost beyond belief.

Shakespeare's overriding concern for design and plot-mechanisms cannot be overlooked as prophecies, curses, warnings, and dreams foretelling the future follow one upon the other, and are recapitulated when they have proved true. Apart from the dramatic irony that the warning is always disregarded, these 'anticipations' and 're-collections' establish a providential design, being normally associated with man's trust in God or in divine retribution: the more such 'anticipations' prove correct the more directly Providence seems to intervene. We thus see that the gradual unfolding of a providential design against the individualist who set himself up against God's order necessitated emphasis upon *character* in the first part of the play, and upon the individualist's improvisations, and then upon *plot* in the second, where the author's design mirrors that of God. We see, further, that Richard's fake piety is not simply a delightful comic touch but prepares us for the central conflict of the play, in which Richard's mighty opposite is not the puppet Richmond but the King of kings. We see, finally, that in a play as antithetically balanced as *Richard III* the hero's defiance of 'the other world' had to be countered by a positive gesture: whether the ghosts (V.3.119 ff.) are 'real' or merely dreams, Richmond's speech before he falls asleep (V.3.109–18) identifies them as a heavenly visitation –

> *O Thou, whose captain I account myself . . .*
> *To Thee I do commend my watchful soul*
> *Ere I let fall the windows of mine eyes.*

Heaven, through the ghosts, effects Richard's moral defeat, and for the individualist that means the end.

Let us now move on from the play's controlling form to some of its other technical devices. If the central conflict involves not Richard and another dramatic character but Richard and God, how and when do we recognize this? How visible is God on the stage? From Richard's first soliloquy, where he introduces himself as 'subtle, false, and treacherous', from his first irrepressible sallies against religion, we anticipate an eventual nemesis. Richard's fake piety, and the emergence of a providential design, reinforce these expectations, but there are other, unmistakable tokens.

'Conscience', for example, has been made one of the play's leading themes, woven through it as through a piece of music. Clarence's apocalyptic dream illustrates the terrible powers of conscience, 'the tempest to my soul' (I.4), and prepares for Richard's twin-dream, where conscience at last overwhelms him (V.3.178 ff.) –

> *Give me another horse! Bind up my wounds!*
> *Have mercy, Jesu! – Soft! I did but dream.*
> *O coward conscience, how dost thou afflict me!*

Between these poetic *tours de force* conscience never slips from view for long. Clarence's two murderers pick it up, and fool around with it ('Where's thy conscience now?' 'O, in the Duke of Gloucester's purse.' 'When he opens his purse to give us our reward, thy conscience flies out'). King Edward, once a gay sinner, dies conscience-smitten, as do others, notably Hastings and Buckingham, when led off to execution. Tyrrel's heightened account of the repentance of Dighton and Forrest, the two 'fleshed villains' who murdered the princes (IV.3.1–23), underlines the miraculous workings of conscience, and was no doubt inserted to make credible Richard's own change in Act V. (The chronicles say nothing about the murderers' remorse.)

For, on waking from his dream, Richard, like a dog licking a wound, cannot leave conscience alone: 'My conscience hath a thousand several tongues', 'Conscience is but a word that cowards use', 'Our strong arms be our conscience, swords our law!' (V.3.194, 310, 312). He now knows his greatest enemy and, as he explains (V.3.217–20), it is not 'shallow Richmond' – who need not be thought a failure as a dramatic antagonist, which he was never intended to be, since he functions only as an avenging angel.

The never-ending procession of churchmen across the stage also has its effect. We encounter an archbishop in II.4, Cardinal Bourchier in III.1, the Bishop of Ely in III.4, two nameless bishops in III.7; we hear of Doctor Shaw and Friar Penker in III.5; by the merest chance Hastings exchanges some casual words with 'a priest' in III.2, and Derby employs 'Sir Christopher Urswick, a Priest' as his messenger to Richmond (IV.5). Quietly but unremittingly the Church goes through its routines in the background of the play's central scenes. The historical fact that some of its high officers tried to serve God and Mammon fitted admirably into Shakespeare's ironic scheme – thus the 'strawberry' incident (III.4.31–47) establishes not only Richard's ascendancy but a bishop's eagerness to please – yet thematically the churchmen also have a vital function. If we remember that, by and large, Shakespeare's stage directions listed only the speaking parts in a scene, we see that even more ecclesiastics are required than I have mentioned. A funeral procession, a coronation, the taking of sanctuary, and several execution scenes (III.3, III.4.80 ff., V.1) punctuate the action, and could all be strengthened atmospherically by silent, black-robed figures. Indirect stage directions seem to hint as much: 'Your friends at Pomfret, they do need the priest'

(III.2.113), 'Make a short shrift; he longs to see your head' (III.4.95). Were I producing the play I would also thread priests into the crowd scenes (II.3, III.1, III.7.54 ff., IV.2, for example), and use the Cross as a sombre prop, even, perhaps, allowing Richard to lean against it absently, to bow to it cynically (I.2.105), or to give it a meaningful pat (III.5.99).

Imagery and vocabulary heighten one's awareness of God. Repeated words, such as heaven, hell, devil, fiend, angel, saint, holy, as also curses and appeals to the Redeemer, set up their reverberations. Various speakers identify Richard as a devil, the son of hell, a dreadful minister of hell, a cacodemon, hell's black intelligencer. The last metaphor suggests that Richard may sometimes wear black – after all, 'Black is the badge of hell' (*Love's Labour's Lost*, IV.3.250). The other diabolic references would drive home the point, yet in plain black he could also melt in among the churchmen when it suited his chameleon purposes – his 'pious' moods, as when he walks 'between two bishops' at III.7.93.

Richard's costume should also bring out a second leading theme. At the end of I.2 he proposes to 'entertain a score or two of tailors'. A producer could choose to ignore this, since the passage is ironical, yet I think that he would be well advised to fit out Richard with at least a new, splendid cloak for his next entrance (I.3.42: there seems to be insufficient time for a complete change), and to provide him later with other 'marvellous proper' clothes. He could thus draw attention to Richard's love of acting and disguise and dissimulation, which is part of the 'appearance and reality' theme. For not only does Richard himself 'seem a saint, when most I play the devil' (I.3.337), the whole play pivots on the irony that man misinterprets the most obvious realities and suckles himself on false appearances. The blind rejection of Queen Margaret's advice in I.3 makes the point with an almost ritual emphasis, while the drawn-out business of the fall of Hastings underscores it heavily with what may be regarded as Shakespeare's most studied series of dramatic ironies, concluded by a summary of all the providential omens that had been left unheeded (III.4.80–93); and of course Richard's indifference to the reality of God is the central irony of the play. I would, accordingly, dress Richard in black in the first two scenes, and again in III.4 and III.7, and elsewhere in whatever costume enables him to masquerade most effectively in his various assumed roles. That Shakespeare himself desired some such reinforcing of the appearance and reality theme through costume we learn from an unusual stage-direction: 'Enter Richard, and Buckingham, in rotten Armour, maruellous ill-fauoured' (III.5.0: see p. 17 above).

While discussing Shakespeare's technique it is necessary to pursue a theme, a symbol or other device in isolation, but as we experience a play all such threads interweave. The two themes that I have mentioned (conscience, appearance and reality) meet in the dreams of Clarence and Derby and the joint dream of Richmond and Richard (I.4.9 ff., III.2.10 ff., V.3.118 ff.), which are themselves linked in their dramatic irony, as also in generating an unforgettable sense of stark panic. Clarence's dream, described by some as the play's poetic centre, is deservedly admired as, technically, a master-stroke of economy. It reflects ironically not only upon Clarence's imminent 'death by water' – or wine – but upon the values to which Richard so zestfully commits himself. What are wedges of gold or heaps of pearl (I.4.26) if not symbols of Richard's royal aspirations? In addition I suspect that the climax of the under-water scene –

34

> *... and in the holes*
> *Where eyes did once inhabit, there were crept,*
> *As 'twere in scorn of eyes, reflecting gems*

– was inspired by Richard's own flashing eyes. 'His eyes whirled about,' says Holinshed (cf. p. 23), and Shakespeare seems to have adopted this idiosyncrasy for he calls Richard 'A cockatrice ... Whose unavoided eye is murderous' (IV.1.54–5), one who owns a 'deadly eye' (I.3.224). Clarence's vision of an after-life, finally, contradicts Richard's irreligion, just as his deeply moving contrition contrasts with Richard's less genuine pangs in the adjoining scenes (I.3.306, II.1.53 ff.).

Style can be studied as another aspect of technique: and the rhetorical artfulness of our play unmistakably solicits attention. Figures of speech are heaped up with a flourish – alliteration, anaphora, antithesis, apostrophe, parallelism, repetition, to name some of the more mechanical favourites.

> *You cloudy princes and heart-sorrowing peers*
> *That bear this heavy mutual load of moan,*
> *Now cheer each other in each other's love.*
> *Though we have spent our harvest of this king,*
> *We are to reap the harvest of his son.*
>
> II.2.112–16

We soon recognize this sort of patterning as a mannerism, and modern readers do not always take to it kindly. If it is any consolation one could inform them that in the literature of the period, and not least in the drama, stylization was all the rage and went to extremes compared with which *Richard III* marks an advance towards naturalism. In the prose and the comedies of John Lyly, the inventor of 'Euphuism', in the Arcadian prose of Sir Philip Sidney, in the tragedies of Kyd and the early Marlowe, an out-

rageously artificial style almost smothered the newly
discovered 'human interest'.

Probably no native author contributed more to the
stylization of English drama than Seneca, the translation
of whose *Ten Tragedies* came out in collected form in 1581,
and was subjected to such 'servile imitation' that Thomas
Nashe warned in 1589 that 'Seneca let blood line by line
and page by page at length must needs die to our stage.'
Nashe was thinking particularly of Seneca's 'sentences' or
moral apophthegms, but much more was pillaged. Seneca's
rhetorical drama specialized in declamation where, as
T. S. Eliot explained, 'the centre of value is shifted from
what the personage says to the way in which he says it'
('Seneca in Elizabethan Translation', in *Selected Essays*,
1951, p. 68). It ranges from reflective and descriptive
speeches that sound, to modern ears, tiresomely long and
bombastic – down to its characteristic stichomythia,
dialogue in alternate single lines or half or quarter lines.
Both of these unnatural speech-forms were adopted by the
Elizabethans, as were others less long or short but equally
conventional. For example, one scene in *Richard III* (IV.4)
contains typical lamentation-speeches, a sustained *persuasio*
full of impersonal sententiousness (line 291), several bouts
of single-line stichomythia (for example, line 343 ff.), and
even one consisting of half-lines (lines 374–7).

The sensationalism of Senecan tragedy also left its
stamp on our play, though perhaps only at second-hand,
through the new Tragedy of Blood. Richard's lip-smack-
ing attitude to death owes more to *The Spanish Tragedy*
and *Tamburlaine* and *Titus Andronicus* than to the
chronicles; details like the carrying on to the stage of
Hastings' head (III.5.20), and the nonchalance of Richard's
'Chop off his head!' (III.1.193, V.3.345), though found in
Holinshed, are lent a special emphasis to bring the action

closer to the Tragedy of Blood, where lives are casually puffed out. To an even greater extent Shakespeare reshaped what he read about Richard's dream before Bosworth: 'it seemed to him being asleep, that he did see diverse images like terrible devils, which pulled and haled him, not suffering him to take any quiet or rest' (Holinshed, p. 755). Senecan ghosts replace the devils and, as in *The Spanish Tragedy* and an early *Hamlet* (c. 1589), they rise to exact revenge.

While the rhetorical rigidities and artifices of *Richard III* seem immature, and reflect the inevitable growing-pains of English drama, the author's personal youthfulness betrays itself in other ways. In *Richard III* he attempted a sophisticated study of man's moral nature. One cannot resist comparing this early play with Shakespeare's supreme tragedies. *Macbeth*, in particular, resumes the same subject, the ambitious man who murders for a crown, and technically resembles *Richard III* all too often – an unusual self-repetition that may indicate Shakespeare's awareness of his earlier inadequacies. Just as the poetry of *Macbeth* soars beyond the reach of the young Shakespeare, the exploration of his hero's mind and conscience in *Richard III*, which has been rightly labelled 'primitive technique', if only because it works at a level not much superior to that of *The Spanish Tragedy*, cannot compete with the intellectual and emotional insights of the tragic period. It is not that Shakespeare was uninterested in these matters but merely that he lacked technical (and perhaps human) experience.

Before dismissing the dramatist's moral perceptiveness as immature one should, however, notice that some of his simplifications can be paralleled in his profoundest plays. For example, he whitewashed Queen Elizabeth, dissociating her from the murder of Clarence (see p. 24), and thus depicted her as entirely virtuous – which suits his schematic

37

design. For the same reason, he exaggerated the simplicity of those who stood in Richard's way, Clarence, the King, Hastings, the two princes, the Lord Mayor, and also the Queen in Acts I–III. In the result the Queen, and Richard's other opponents, are morally 'reduced' to a less than human size. But, as I have said, the same thing happens to moral issues and minor characters in later tragedies like *Macbeth*. In Holinshed, Macbeth thinks he has a just quarrel in seizing the throne, and Duncan is described as an ineffective and Macbeth as a good king: Shakespeare straightened out some such moral nodosities, and also resorted to crude moralizing and choric scenes such as II.4 (Ross and an Old Man) or III.6 (Lennox and another Lord), which cannot be considered a great advance on *Richard III* II.3 (the meeting of citizens) and III.6 (the Scrivener).

A mature tragedy, no less than an early experimental one, may have to scale down minor characters in these ways, and clarify *some* moral obscurities. The test of its morality is to be found in its central experiences, which either illuminate the mystery in human relationships (as, pre-eminently, in *Othello*), or 'the horror, the horror' (as Conrad called it in *Heart of Darkness*) when human nature becomes a law unto itself (as, at different levels, in *Hamlet* and *Macbeth*). The two types may of course combine in a single play, but it can be seen at a glance that *Richard III* belongs to the second and, being Shakespeare's first attempt in this tragic mode, fails – by the highest standards. It fails because Richard's wit at first screens off the full horror of his moral nature, and later, when his intellectual confidence finally collapses, one makes no profound discoveries about human nature since his has been reduced to that of a rat in a trap. Whereas in Marlowe's twin-study of intellectual arrogance, *Doctor Faustus*, the poetry of the hero's last speech burns with moral feeling, Richard's last great speech (V.3.178 ff.: 'Give me another horse! Bind up my wounds!...') is merely theatrical, its morality mere rhetoric. It is not entirely unfair, I think, to compare his perfunctory 'Have mercy, Jesu!' (V.3.179) with Faustus' more agonized cry –

> *See, see where Christ's blood streams in the firmament!*
> *One drop would save my soul, half a drop. Ah, my Christ!*

Richard, like Faustus, fights a losing battle with his God, but Shakespeare could not allow his doomed hero to appeal so powerfully to the audience: from the very outset he had chosen to write a theatrical rather than an inward-gazing moral tragedy.

Yet, though Shakespeare had not achieved his mature insight into man's moral nature, a gift as precious as his poetry and his other dramatic skills, there are signs of what was to come. Richard may be the melodramatic villain in many of his best scenes; nevertheless, our attitude to him should not be one of mere loathing. On the contrary: correctly produced, he must compel admiration – not only his verbal and intellectual agility but his artistic gifts and, at times, his clowning, should positively delight us. Unless we recognize that Shakespeare put a good deal of himself into Richard's theatrical genius we shall not understand the villain's attractiveness, nor his curious, inverted affinity to the Prince of Denmark, the other Shakespearian hero with a connoisseur's sense of theatre. Our essentially mixed response to Richard involves us in his moral nature – not during his soliloquies, where Shakespeare's mature tragic heroes enthral us most completely, but whenever he is convincingly a human being and combines mercurial wit and evil (for example, II.1.47 ff., III.4.59 ff., III.7.94 ff., IV.2.82 ff.).

Some other instances of an ambivalent moral awareness may now be mentioned. Whereas many of the characters are neatly defined as good or bad, a few escape this schematism. The most notable is Queen Margaret, a modernized Cassandra, the only person in the play who matches Richard in strength of will, in total self-absorption, and in her understanding of history. We are not allowed to forget her past as a sadist and an instigator of child-murder, and in particular her offer of a rag to the Duke of York 'Steeped in the faultless blood of pretty Rutland' (I.3.173 ff., IV.4.44–5). Shakespeare thus emphasizes her resemblance to Richard, yet at the same time he brings out fully the pathos of her position. The real Queen Margaret had in fact left England in 1475, and died in 1482, prior to the main action of the play. Shakespeare's Margaret may therefore be regarded as his most important addition to the story. She contributes to it not only as Richard's 'reflector' but also as the pivot of an unsophisticated tit-for-tat morality connecting past, present, and future. Her curses and prophecies in I.3 have a function in some ways similar to that of the prophecies in *Macbeth*. Yet, justly admired though she is, Queen Margaret, a too thinly disguised chorus, must rate as apprentice-work, with her stereotyped speeches and her improbable comings and goings. What an immense distance Shakespeare travelled from the wailing women of *Richard III* to the Weird Sisters!

The Earl of Derby differs from Queen Margaret in that his moral commitments are only gradually disclosed. At his first entrance the Queen challenges him as a potential enemy, and he answers unconvincingly (I.3). By II.2.100, the stage direction 'Enter Richard, Buckingham, Derby, Hastings, and Ratcliffe' identifies him as one of Richard's party, though he remains significantly silent. He next puzzles us as the timorous dreamer (III.2), then as a by-stander when his friend Hastings is sent to the block (III.4). In IV.1 he seems at first to have accepted a role as one of Richard's cat's-paws, till his sensible warning to Dorset (line 48) proves him not quite so passive. Derby, it must be made abundantly clear, is not just 'another Lord', little though he has to do in his first scenes. He is a hardening moral force, and he bides his time – like Albany in *King Lear*.

King Edward, Clarence, and Hastings also invite an ambivalent response, but no character in the play, apart from Richard, acts upon our moral equilibrium quite as disturbingly as one person just outside it. To Shore's wife, successively the mistress of King Edward and of Hastings, Shakespeare assigned what may appear a place of un-necessary prominence in the opening scene (I.1.71–102). Having 'planted' her, he briefly jogs our memories (III.1.184–5) in preparation for Richard's violent accusa-tions against 'that harlot, strumpet Shore', 'this damnèd strumpet' (III.4.71, 74), and later reflections on Hastings' 'apparent open guilt ... I mean, his conversation with Shore's wife' (III.5.30–31, 50). The lady's infamy, be it observed, becomes a moral touchstone. Whenever Richard refers to it we feel that he is manipulating normal moral attitudes to mask much more serious crimes, the murders of Clarence and Hastings. Precisely the same happens when he and his echo Buckingham indict King Edward's 'hateful luxury | And bestial appetite' (III.5.79 ff., III.7.7), which again involves Mistress Shore: hypocritically in-dignant about lust, Richard plans to usurp the crown and, already perhaps, to murder his nephews. The effect of this awareness is that we incline to forgive Mistress Shore, partly because Richard condemns her. Significantly, too, representatives of common opinion call the two men who share her guilt 'good King Edward' (Third Citizen, II.3.7) and 'the good Lord Hastings' (the Scrivener, III.6.1), and both men are depicted as well-intentioned (Hastings' ingenuous loyalty to 'my master's heirs', III.2.54, which we know will cost him his head, more than compensates for his spitefulness about his enemies). Mistress Shore, characterized by association, therefore contrasts with Richard as an essentially harmless immoralist: we are entitled to compare Richard's two detestable wooing-scenes and her fornication with King Edward and Hastings, though Shakespeare refrains from doing so. In Act III the mere mention of Mistress Shore intensifies our uneasiness about official morality and its priorities. Her function, in short, is the same as that of the invisible Falstaff in *Henry V*.

While *Richard III* must be seen as an apprentice-piece compared with Shakespeare's best tragedies, it nevertheless possesses 'moral dimensions' to which they cannot pretend. Coming after the three parts of *Henry VI*, *Richard III* concludes Shakespeare's first tetralogy of history plays, his panorama of the Wars of the Roses, and so knits together a greater variety of threads than any single drama. (Richard, like his two brothers, appears in the last three plays of the tetralogy, and Queen Margaret in all four.) In this larger framework Richard's treacheries represent not only the wickedness of an individual but the residual evil of a family, and of England, two larger bodies that can be purged only when they expel the poison (I.3.245, 290, etc.) that is Richard.

The ramifications of the family are more intricate than in *Hamlet* or *King Lear*, and create a richer image of the past. A sense of community, both of man with his fellows and of the present with the past and future, emerges, indeed, as one of the fundamental spiritual forces against

which Richard engages himself. In the eyes of Shakespeare's contemporaries this sense would be closely linked
to their Christianity – what is religion if not a 'binding
together'? – so that Richard's unnaturalness to his family
and his country would seem to follow logically from his
atheism. Shakespeare, accordingly, stressed the sense of
community, just as he did the other 'religious' implica-
tions, making of it a dynamic more than equal to Richard's
own. We should feel its mysterious power when the three
royal widows set aside their differences, their murdered
husbands and sons – united in their hatred of Richard
(IV.4); and even more shatteringly, when Richard's own
mother curses him, formally, at what she knows to be their
last meeting (IV.4.184), and he has no reply. Or again, at a
less solemn moment, we feel the mystery when Hastings
meets another Hastings and recalls how they once met on
the same spot in, as he thinks, less happy circumstances –
though in fact the circumstances are also the same
(III.2.94–106).

> *Ere Babylon was dust*
> *The Magus Zoroaster, my dead child,*
> *Met his own image walking in the garden. . . .*

Yet, though a sense of community plays so decisive a part,
it can be overemphasized. E. M. W. Tillyard has contended
that 'In spite of the eminence of Richard's character
the main business of the play is to complete the national
tetralogy and to display the working out of God's plan
to restore England to prosperity' (*Shakespeare's History
Plays*, p. 199). This is to take the 'tetralogy' altogether too
seriously. Shakespeare, so far as we can tell, did nothing to
make his tetralogies available as such, either in print or in
the theatre. Like the other dramatists of his time he had to
plan even two-part plays largely, if not entirely, as two

self-contained units: for *Richard III*, as I have tried to show, he devised a firm internal structure, totally different from the loosely episodic sequences of *Henry VI*. Themes and characters may survive from earlier histories, but do so only when relevant to more immediate purposes. *Richard III*, the first English play that has consistently held the stage, stands triumphantly on its own.

*

That, at least, is a modern view. For well over a hundred years, it must be added, the play was less highly regarded, in so far as it was not acted in Shakespeare's version but in a patchwork adaptation by Colley Cibber, first performed at Drury Lane in 1700. In this text Clarence's dream and Queen Margaret's curse and much else disappeared, and the dialogue was padded with extracts from *Henry VI*, *Richard II*, *Henry IV*, and *Henry V*, as also with some 'original' Cibber ('Off with his head; so much for Buckingham'). Kemble revised Cibber's adaptation in 1811, reverting to Shakespeare's language here and there; and a production of 1821, with Macready as Richard, swept away more of Cibber's interpolations, without fully restoring Shakespeare's text. Only Queen Margaret's first scene was given in 1821. The next 'back to Shakespeare' movement (Phelps, 1845), cleared away more Cibber, and sanctioned Queen Margaret's second scene. According to the reviewer of *The Times* this improved the play decisively. '[Queen Margaret] gives unity to the play. . . . She is the incarnate Nemesis, – the revelation of Fate, – almost the Chorus of the play. Mrs Warner played her admirably. She entered with the aspect less of a human enemy than of some supernatural being. The intensity and violence of her hate were terrific.' Later, however, Phelps revived Cibber's version (1861–2), as did Charles Kean; and when

Henry Irving once more repudiated Cibber (1877), he simultaneously threw out so much genuine Shakespeare (for example, Queen Margaret's second scene, and large parts of Clarence's dream and murder) that the story lost much of its coherence.

Some credit for the popularity of *Richard III* from 1700 onwards must therefore go to Cibber; and even in the twentieth century Cibberian touches are not disdained, as Laurence Olivier's film illustrates all too clearly. But, though it has been claimed, by no less an authority than G. C. D. Odell (see Further Reading), that Cibber's more melodramatic version 'acts better' than Shakespeare's, and deserved its success in keeping the authentic text from the public, it should be stressed that greater plays than *Richard III* suffered the same fate. Tate's adaptation of *King Lear* was almost as long-lived as Cibber's *Richard III*. These versions, no doubt, indicate some dissatisfaction with the originals, yet their success can also be seen as a tribute to the originals, misguided but well-intentioned. In one form or another, 'Shakespeare's *Richard III*' was always in demand.

FURTHER READING

Criticism

THE outstanding critical study of the play, W. H. Clemen's *A Commentary on Shakespeare's Richard III* (1968), first published in German (Göttingen 1957), is now available in English, and there are several books on the Histories with useful chapters on *Richard III*: E. M. W. Tillyard, *Shakespeare's History Plays* (1944; Peregrine Books 1962), Irving Ribner, *The English History Play in the Age of Shakespeare* (1957, 1965), M. M. Reese, *The Cease of Majesty: A Study of Shakespeare's History Plays* (1961), Robert Ornstein, *A Kingdom for a Stage: The Achievement of Shakespeare's History Plays* (Harvard University Press 1972). Emrys Jones, *The Origins of Shakespeare* (Oxford 1977) deals only with the early Histories, and is particularly good on *Richard III*. Lily B. Campbell, *Shakespeare's 'Histories': Mirrors of Elizabethan Policy* (San Marino 1947), and S. C. Sen Gupta, *Shakespeare's Historical Plays* (1964), also deserve mention. Editions of the play, most general books on Shakespeare, and many on Shakespearian tragedy, deal with *Richard III*, more or less fully, and other excellent critical essays may be found in the periodicals: A. P. Rossiter, 'The Structure of *Richard III*' (*Durham University Journal*, 1938) (see also Rossiter, 'The Unity of *Richard III*' in *Angel with Horns*, 1961; reprinted in *Shakespeare's Histories: An Anthology of Modern Criticism*, edited by William A. Armstrong, Penguin Shakespeare Library, 1972); R. A. Law, '*Richard the Third*: A Study in Shakespeare's Composition' (*Publications of the Modern Language Association of America*, 1945); W. H. Clemen, 'Anticipation and Foreboding in Shakespeare's Early Histories' (*Shakespeare Survey 6*, 1953);

N. Brooke, 'Tragedy versus History in *Richard III*' (*Critical Quarterly*, 1965); A. L. French, 'The World of Richard III' (*Shakespeare Studies* IV, 1968); Waldo F. McNeir, 'The Masks of Richard the Third' (*Studies in English Literature* XI, 1971), A. Gurr, 'Richard III and the Democratic Process' (*Essays in Criticism*, 1974). There are valuable chapters on *Richard III* in Wilbur Sanders, *The Dramatist and the Received Idea* (Cambridge 1968), and in Nicholas Brooke, *Shakespeare's Early Tragedies* (1968).

Editions

Modern textual studies of the play began with Peter Alexander, *Shakespeare's 'Henry VI' and 'Richard III'* (Cambridge 1929), E. K. Chambers, *William Shakespeare* (2 vols., Oxford 1930), and D. L. Patrick, *The Textual History of 'Richard III'* (Stanford University 1936). Sir Walter Greg, in his monumental work on Shakespeare's text, *The Shakespeare First Folio* (Oxford 1955), agreed with Patrick's views about the Quarto, but the relative merits of the Quarto and Folio texts are now interpreted somewhat differently: compare Alice Walker, *Textual Problems of the First Folio* (Cambridge 1953), J. K. Walton, *The Quarto Copy for the First Folio of Shakespeare* (Dublin University Press, 1971), A. S. Cairncross, 'The Quarto and the Folio Text of *Richard III*' (*Review of English Studies*, 1957), E. A. J. Honigmann, 'The Text of *Richard III*' (*Theatre Research*, 1965), and 'On the Indifferent and One-Way Variants in Shakespeare' (*The Library*, 1967), K. P. Wentersdorf, '*Richard III* (Q1) and the Pembroke "Bad" Quartos' (*English Language Notes*, 1977). Kristian Smidt has prepared a useful edition of the play with parallel texts of the Quarto and Folio (Oslo and New York, 1969). Synthetic texts prepared by recent British editors (P. Alexander, 1951; C. J. Sisson, 1954; J. D. Wilson, 1954) therefore vary in many readings.

Background Material

Kenneth Muir's *The Sources of Shakespeare's Plays* (1977) gives the latest survey of the sources of *Richard III*. Geoffrey Bullough, in *Narrative and Dramatic Sources of Shakespeare*, volume III (1960), also surveys the play's sources, and reprints the most important ones. Reprints may also be found in *Shakespeare's Holinshed: An Edition of Holinshed's Chronicles (1587)*, selected, edited, and annotated by Richard Hosley (New York 1968), and, in old spelling, in W. G. Boswell-Stone *Shakespere's Holinshed* (1896), and H. H. Furness, Jr, *Richard III*, A New Variorum Edition (1908). J. D. Wilson in his valuable edition (Cambridge 1954), Clemen (*Commentary*), R. A. Law (as above), and H. H. Glunz, *Shakespeare und Morus* (Bochum 1938), all discuss the sources in some detail. The two different theories about the relationship of *Richard III* and *The True Tragedy of Richard III* are explained by J. D. Wilson (*Shakespeare Quarterly*, 1952) and E. A. J. Honigmann (*Modern Language Review*, 1954).

For the general evolution of the story of Richard III before Shakespeare the best guide is G. B. Churchill, *Richard the Third up to Shakespeare* (Berlin 1900: *Palaestra* X). More modern estimates of the historical Richard are offered by E. F. Jacob, *The Fifteenth Century 1399–1485* (The Oxford History of England, Oxford 1961), and by one of Richard's several apologists, P. M. Kendall (*Richard the Third*, 1955). Alison Hanham's *Richard III and his early historians* (Oxford 1975) examines Richard's early reputation, and the connections between early sources. Peter Saccio has written a book of particular value to students of Shakespeare, in which he compares Shakespeare's view of history with that of Tudor chroniclers and of modern historians (*Shakespeare's English Kings: History, Chronicle, and Drama*, Oxford 1977).

Alice I. P. Wood, *The Stage History of Shakespeare's King Richard the Third* (New York 1909), deals with the play's theatrical fortunes in England and America. G. C. D. Odell, *Shakespeare from Betterton to Irving* (2 vols., 1921), covers the same ground, and, in the section on stage-history in J. D. Wilson's edition, C. B. Young does so again, and then advances into the twentieth century. Cibber's play can be read in *Five*

KING RICHARD THE THIRD

THE CHARACTERS IN THE PLAY

KING EDWARD IV

EDWARD, Prince of Wales, afterwards King Edward V } sons of King Edward

RICHARD, Duke of York

GEORGE, Duke of Clarence

RICHARD, Duke of Gloucester, after- } brothers of King
   wards King Richard III   Edward

QUEEN ELIZABETH, wife of King Edward

DUCHESS OF YORK, mother of King Edward and his
   brothers

LADY ANNE, widow of Edward, Prince of Wales, the son
   of King Henry VI; afterwards married to Richard, Duke
   of Gloucester

EDWARD PLANTAGENET } children of Clarence
MARGARET PLANTAGENET

QUEEN MARGARET, widow of King Henry VI

HENRY, Earl of Richmond, afterwards King Henry VII

CARDINAL (Thomas Bourchier, Archbishop of Canter-
   bury)

ARCHBISHOP (Thomas Rotheram, Archbishop of York)

JOHN MORTON, Bishop of Ely

DUKE OF BUCKINGHAM

DUKE OF NORFOLK

EARL OF SURREY, son of Norfolk

EARL OF OXFORD

ANTHONY WOODVILLE, Earl Rivers, brother of Queen
   Elizabeth

MARQUESS OF DORSET
LORD GREY } sons of Queen Elizabeth
EARL OF DERBY (also called Lord Stanley)
LORD HASTINGS
LORD LOVEL
SIR RICHARD RATCLIFFE
SIR WILLIAM CATESBY
SIR JAMES TYRREL
SIR THOMAS VAUGHAN
SIR JAMES BLUNT
SIR WALTER HERBERT
SIR WILLIAM BRANDON
SIR ROBERT BRAKENBURY, Lieutenant of the Tower
KEEPER in the Tower
CHRISTOPHER URSWICK, a Priest
JOHN, another Priest
TRESSEL, BERKELEY, gentlemen attending on Lady Anne
LORD MAYOR of London
SHERIFF of Wiltshire
GHOSTS of King Henry VI, Edward Prince of Wales, and
    other victims of Richard
HASTINGS, a Pursuivant
Scrivener
Page
Two Murderers
Lords and other Attendants
Messengers, Soldiers, Bishops, Aldermen, Citizens

BUT, polext wond. transition

Handwritten annotations:

Convention of Jacobean plays
↓
Prologue / chorus / intro. like
Dionysius

Enter Richard, Duke of Gloucester, alone   **I.1**

RICHARD   *talks to audience*

Now is the winter of our discontent
Made glorious summer by this sun of York, *Plantagenet family*
And all the clouds that loured upon our house
In the deep bosom of the ocean buried. *including ? audience.*
                               public
Now are our brows bound with victorious wreaths,
Our bruisèd arms hung up for monuments,
Our stern alarums changed to merry meetings,
Our dreadful marches to delightful measures.
Grim-visaged war hath smoothed his wrinkled front,
And now, instead of mounting barbèd steeds   **10**
To fright the souls of fearful adversaries,
He capers nimbly in a lady's chamber
To the lascivious pleasing of a lute.
large But I, that am not shaped for sportive tricks   *transition*
Nor made to court an amorous looking-glass;
I, that am rudely stamped, and want love's majesty
To strut before a wanton ambling nymph;
I, that am curtailed of this fair proportion,
Cheated of feature by dissembling Nature,   *private*
Deformed, unfinished, sent before my time   **20**
Into this breathing world, scarce half made up,
And that so lamely and unfashionable
That dogs bark at me as I halt by them –
Why I, in this weak piping time of peace,
Have no delight to pass away the time,

[approximation to intimacy]
film - need to hear us.

Unless to spy my shadow in the sun
And descant on mine own deformity.
And therefore, since I cannot prove a lover
To entertain these fair well-spoken days,
30 I am determined to prove a villain
And hate the idle pleasures of these days.
Plots have I laid, inductions dangerous,
By drunken prophecies, libels, and dreams,
To set my brother Clarence and the King
In deadly hate the one against the other;
And if King Edward be as true and just
As I am subtle, false, and treacherous,
This day should Clarence closely be mewed up
About a prophecy which says that G –
40 Of Edward's heirs the murderer shall be.
Dive, thoughts, down to my soul – here Clarence comes!
    Enter Clarence, guarded, and Brakenbury, Lieutenant
    of the Tower
Brother, good day. What means this armèd guard
That waits upon your grace?

CLARENCE   His majesty,
Tendering my person's safety, hath appointed
This conduct to convey me to the Tower.

RICHARD
Upon what cause?

CLARENCE   Because my name is George.

RICHARD
Alack, my lord, that fault is none of yours,
He should for that commit your godfathers.
O, belike his majesty hath some intent
50 That you should be new-christened in the Tower.
But what's the matter, Clarence, may I know?

CLARENCE
Yea, Richard, when I know; for I protest

56

As yet I do not. But, as I can learn,
He hearkens after prophecies and dreams,
And from the cross-row plucks the letter G,
And says a wizard told him that by G
His issue disinherited should be.
And, for my name of George begins with G,
It follows in his thought that I am he.
These, as I learn, and such-like toys as these   60
Hath moved his highness to commit me now.

RICHARD

Why this it is when men are ruled by women;
'Tis not the King that sends you to the Tower.
My Lady Grey his wife, Clarence, 'tis she
That tempers him to this extremity.
Was it not she, and that good man of worship,
Anthony Woodville, her brother there,
That made him send Lord Hastings to the Tower,
From whence this present day he is delivered?
We are not safe, Clarence, we are not safe.   70

CLARENCE

By heaven, I think there is no man secure
But the Queen's kindred, and night-walking heralds
That trudge betwixt the King and Mistress Shore.
Heard you not what an humble suppliant
Lord Hastings was for his delivery?

RICHARD

Humbly complaining to her deity
Got my Lord Chamberlain his liberty.
I'll tell you what, I think it is our way,
If we will keep in favour with the King,
To be her men and wear her livery.   80
The jealous o'erworn widow and herself,
Since that our brother dubbed them gentlewomen,
Are mighty gossips in this monarchy.

BRAKENBURY

> I beseech your graces both to pardon me.
> His majesty hath straitly given in charge
> That no man shall have private conference,
> Of what degree soever, with his brother.

RICHARD

> Even so? An't please your worship, Brakenbury,
> You may partake of anything we say.
> We speak no treason, man; we say the King
> Is wise and virtuous, and his noble Queen
> Well struck in years, fair, and not jealous;
> We say that Shore's wife hath a pretty foot,
> A cherry lip, a bonny eye, a passing pleasing tongue;
> And that the Queen's kindred are made gentlefolks.
> How say you, sir? Can you deny all this?

BRAKENBURY

> With this, my lord, myself have naught to do.

RICHARD

> Naught to do with Mistress Shore? I tell thee, fellow,
> He that doth naught with her, excepting one,
> Were best he do it secretly, alone.

BRAKENBURY

> What one, my lord?

RICHARD

> Her husband, knave. Wouldst thou betray me?

BRAKENBURY

> I do beseech your grace to pardon me, and withal
> Forbear your conference with the noble Duke.

CLARENCE

> We know thy charge, Brakenbury, and will obey.

RICHARD

> We are the Queen's abjects, and must obey.
> Brother, farewell. I will unto the King;

And whatsoe'er you will employ me in,
Were it to call King Edward's widow sister,
I will perform it to enfranchise you.   110
Meantime, this deep disgrace in brotherhood
Touches me deeper than you can imagine.

CLARENCE
I know it pleaseth neither of us well.

RICHARD
Well, your imprisonment shall not be long:
I will deliver you, or else lie for you.
Meantime, have patience.

CLARENCE   I must perforce. Farewell.
                    Exit Clarence with Brakenbury and guard

RICHARD
Go, tread the path that thou shalt ne'er return.
Simple plain Clarence, I do love thee so
That I will shortly send thy soul to heaven,
If heaven will take the present at our hands.   120
But who comes here? The new-delivered Hastings?
        Enter Lord Hastings

HASTINGS
Good time of day unto my gracious lord.

RICHARD
As much unto my good Lord Chamberlain.
Well are you welcome to the open air.
How hath your lordship brooked imprisonment?

HASTINGS
With patience, noble lord, as prisoners must;
But I shall live, my lord, to give them thanks
That were the cause of my imprisonment.

RICHARD
No doubt, no doubt; and so shall Clarence too,
For they that were your enemies are his,   130

59

And have prevailed as much on him as you.

HASTINGS

More pity that the eagles should be mewed,
Whiles kites and buzzards prey at liberty.

RICHARD

What news abroad?

HASTINGS

No news so bad abroad as this at home:
The King is sickly, weak, and melancholy,
And his physicians fear him mightily.

RICHARD

Now, by Saint John, that news is bad indeed!
O, he hath kept an evil diet long

140 And over-much consumed his royal person.
'Tis very grievous to be thought upon.
Where is he? In his bed?

HASTINGS

He is.

RICHARD

Go you before, and I will follow you.   *Exit Hastings*
He cannot live, I hope, and must not die
Till George be packed with post-horse up to heaven.
I'll in, to urge his hatred more to Clarence
With lies well steeled with weighty arguments;
And, if I fail not in my deep intent,

150 Clarence hath not another day to live;
Which done, God take King Edward to His mercy
And leave the world for me to bustle in!
For then I'll marry Warwick's youngest daughter.
What though I killed her husband and her father?
The readiest way to make the wench amends
Is to become her husband and her father,
The which will I – not all so much for love
As for another secret close intent

By marrying her which I must reach unto.
But yet I run before my horse to market: 160
Clarence still breathes; Edward still lives and reigns;
When they are gone, then must I count my gains. *Exit*

Enter the corse of Henry the Sixth, with halberds to **I.2**
guard it; Lady Anne being the mourner, attended by
Tressel and Berkeley

ANNE

Set down, set down your honourable load –
If honour may be shrouded in a hearse –
Whilst I awhile obsequiously lament
Th'untimely fall of virtuous Lancaster.
    The bearers set down the hearse
Poor key-cold figure of a holy king,
Pale ashes of the house of Lancaster,
Thou bloodless remnant of that royal blood,
Be it lawful that I invocate thy ghost
To hear the lamentations of poor Anne,
Wife to thy Edward, to thy slaughtered son   10
Stabbed by the selfsame hand that made these wounds!
Lo, in these windows that let forth thy life
I pour the helpless balm of my poor eyes.
O, cursèd be the hand that made these holes!
Cursèd the heart that had the heart to do it!
Cursèd the blood that let this blood from hence!
More direful hap betide that hated wretch
That makes us wretched by the death of thee
Than I can wish to wolves – to spiders, toads,
Or any creeping venomed thing that lives!   20
If ever he have child, abortive be it,
Prodigious, and untimely brought to light,
Whose ugly and unnatural aspect

May fright the hopeful mother at the view,
And that be heir to his unhappiness!
If ever he have wife, let her be made
More miserable by the life of him
Than I am made by my young lord and thee!
Come now, towards Chertsey with your holy load,
30 Taken from Paul's to be interrèd there.
> *The bearers take up the hearse*
And still, as you are weary of this weight,
Rest you, whiles I lament King Henry's corse.
> *Enter Richard, Duke of Gloucester*

RICHARD
Stay, you that bear the corse, and set it down.

ANNE
What black magician conjures up this fiend
To stop devoted charitable deeds?

RICHARD
Villains, set down the corse, or, by Saint Paul,
I'll make a corse of him that disobeys!

GENTLEMAN
My lord, stand back, and let the coffin pass.

RICHARD
Unmannered dog! Stand thou, when I command!
40 Advance thy halberd higher than my breast,
Or, by Saint Paul, I'll strike thee to my foot
And spurn upon thee, beggar, for thy boldness.
> *The bearers set down the hearse*

ANNE
What, do you tremble? Are you all afraid?
Alas, I blame you not, for you are mortal,
And mortal eyes cannot endure the devil.
Avaunt, thou dreadful minister of hell!
Thou hadst but power over his mortal body;
His soul thou canst not have. Therefore, be gone.

RICHARD

Sweet saint, for charity, be not so curst.

ANNE

Foul devil, for God's sake hence, and trouble us not, 50
For thou hast made the happy earth thy hell,
Filled it with cursing cries and deep exclaims.
If thou delight to view thy heinous deeds,
Behold this pattern of thy butcheries.
O gentlemen, see, see! Dead Henry's wounds
Open their congealed mouths and bleed afresh!
Blush, blush, thou lump of foul deformity;
For 'tis thy presence that exhales this blood
From cold and empty veins where no blood dwells.
Thy deeds inhuman and unnatural 60
Provokes this deluge most unnatural.
O God, which this blood mad'st, revenge his death!
O earth, which this blood drink'st, revenge his death!
Either heaven with lightning strike the murderer dead;
Or earth gape open wide and eat him quick,
As thou dost swallow up this good King's blood
Which his hell-governed arm hath butcherèd!

RICHARD

Lady, you know no rules of charity,
Which renders good for bad, blessings for curses.

ANNE

Villain, thou know'st nor law of God nor man: 70
No beast so fierce but knows some touch of pity.

RICHARD

But I know none, and therefore am no beast.

ANNE

O wonderful, when devils tell the truth!

RICHARD

More wonderful, when angels are so angry.
Vouchsafe, divine perfection of a woman,

Of these supposèd crimes to give me leave
By circumstance but to acquit myself.

ANNE

Vouchsafe, diffused infection of a man,
Of these known evils, but to give me leave
By circumstance to accuse thy cursèd self.

RICHARD

Fairer than tongue can name thee, let me have
Some patient leisure to excuse myself.

ANNE

Fouler than heart can think thee, thou canst make
No excuse current but to hang thyself.

RICHARD

By such despair I should accuse myself.

ANNE

And by despairing shalt thou stand excused
For doing worthy vengeance on thyself
That didst unworthy slaughter upon others.

RICHARD

Say that I slew them not?

ANNE   Then say they were not slain.

But dead they are, and, devilish slave, by thee.

RICHARD

I did not kill your husband.

ANNE   Why, then he is alive.

RICHARD

Nay, he is dead, and slain by Edward's hands.

ANNE

In thy foul throat thou li'st! Queen Margaret saw
Thy murderous falchion smoking in his blood;
The which thou once didst bend against her breast,
But that thy brothers beat aside the point.

RICHARD

I was provokèd by her slanderous tongue

64

That laid their guilt upon my guiltless shoulders.

ANNE

Thou wast provokèd by thy bloody mind
That never dream'st on aught but butcheries. 100
Didst thou not kill this King?

RICHARD I grant ye – yea.

ANNE

Dost grant me, hedgehog? Then God grant me too
Thou mayst be damnèd for that wicked deed!
O, he was gentle, mild, and virtuous!

RICHARD

The better for the King of Heaven that hath him.

ANNE

He is in heaven, where thou shalt never come.

RICHARD

Let him thank me that holp to send him thither;
For he was fitter for that place than earth.

ANNE

And thou unfit for any place, but hell.

RICHARD

Yes, one place else, if you will hear me name it. 110

ANNE

Some dungeon.

RICHARD Your bedchamber.

ANNE

Ill rest betide the chamber where thou liest!

RICHARD

So will it, madam, till I lie with you.

ANNE

I hope so.

RICHARD I know so. But, gentle Lady Anne,
To leave this keen encounter of our wits
And fall something into a slower method,
Is not the causer of the timeless deaths

Las to be physically dynamic

Of these Plantagenets, Henry and Edward,
As blameful as the executioner?

ANNE

120   Thou wast the cause and most accursed effect.

RICHARD

Your beauty was the cause of that effect –
Your beauty, that did haunt me in my sleep
To undertake the death of all the world,
So I might live one hour in your sweet bosom.

ANNE

If I thought that, I tell thee, homicide,
These nails should rent that beauty from my cheeks.

RICHARD

These eyes could not endure that beauty's wrack;
You should not blemish it, if I stood by.
As all the world is cheerèd by the sun,

130   So I by that. It is my day, my life.

ANNE

Black night o'ershade thy day, and death thy life!

RICHARD

Curse not thyself, fair creature – thou art both.

ANNE

I would I were, to be revenged on thee.

RICHARD

It is a quarrel most unnatural
To be revenged on him that loveth thee.

ANNE

It is a quarrel just and reasonable
To be revenged on him that killed my husband.

RICHARD

He that bereft thee, lady, of thy husband
Did it to help thee to a better husband.

ANNE

140   His better doth not breathe upon the earth.

RICHARD

He lives, that loves thee better than he could.

ANNE

Name him.

RICHARD   Plantagenet.

ANNE   Why that was he.

RICHARD

The selfsame name, but one of better nature.

ANNE

Where is he?

RICHARD   Here.   — *has to turn to advantage.*

She spits at him

                    Why dost thou spit at me?

ANNE

Would it were mortal poison for thy sake!

RICHARD

Never came poison from so sweet a place.

ANNE

Never hung poison on a fouler toad.

Out of my sight! Thou dost infect mine eyes.

RICHARD

Thine eyes, sweet lady, have infected mine.

ANNE

Would they were basilisks to strike thee dead!   150

RICHARD

I would they were, that I might die at once,

For now they kill me with a living death.

Those eyes of thine from mine have drawn salt tears,

Shamed their aspects with store of childish drops.

These eyes, which never shed remorseful tear –

No, when my father York and Edward wept

To hear the piteous moan that Rutland made

When black-faced Clifford shook his sword at him;

Nor when thy warlike father, like a child,

Richard turns everything to his
advantage
keeps undermining Anne's impetus

160 Told the sad story of my father's death
And twenty times made pause to sob and weep,
That all the standers-by had wet their cheeks
Like trees bedashed with rain – in that sad time
My manly eyes did scorn an humble tear;
And what these sorrows could not thence exhale,
Thy beauty hath, and made them blind with weeping.
I never sued to friend nor enemy;
My tongue could never learn sweet smoothing word;
But, now thy beauty is proposed my fee,
170 My proud heart sues, and prompts my tongue to speak.
        She looks scornfully at him
Teach not thy lip such scorn; for it was made
For kissing, lady, not for such contempt.
If thy revengeful heart cannot forgive,
Lo, here I lend thee this sharp-pointed sword,
Which if thou please to hide in this true breast
And let the soul forth that adoreth thee,
I lay it naked to the deadly stroke
And humbly beg the death upon my knee.
        He lays his breast open. She offers at it with his sword
Nay, do not pause; for I did kill King Henry –
180 But 'twas thy beauty that provokèd me.
Nay now, dispatch; 'twas I that stabbed young Edward –
But 'twas thy heavenly face that set me on.
        She falls the sword
Take up the sword again, or take up me.

ANNE
Arise, dissembler; though I wish thy death
I will not be thy executioner.

RICHARD
Then bid me kill myself, and I will do it.

ANNE
I have already.

68

RICHARD   That was in thy rage.
  Speak it again, and even with the word
  This hand, which for thy love did kill thy love,
  Shall for thy love kill a far truer love;   190
  To both their deaths shalt thou be accessory.

ANNE
  I would I knew thy heart.

RICHARD
  'Tis figured in my tongue.

ANNE
  I fear me both are false.

RICHARD
  Then never was man true.

ANNE
  Well, well, put up your sword.

RICHARD
  Say then my peace is made.

ANNE
  That shalt thou know hereafter.

RICHARD
  But shall I live in hope?

ANNE
  All men, I hope, live so.   200

RICHARD
  Vouchsafe to wear this ring.

ANNE
  To take is not to give.
    She puts on the ring

RICHARD
  Look how my ring encompasseth thy finger,
  Even so thy breast encloseth my poor heart.
  Wear both of them, for both of them are thine;
  And if thy poor devoted servant may
  But beg one favour at thy gracious hand,

defence collapses – automaton.

Thou dost confirm his happiness for ever.

ANNE

What is it?

RICHARD

210   That it may please you leave these sad designs
To him that hath more cause to be a mourner,
And presently repair to Crosby House;
Where, after I have solemnly interred
At Chertsey monastery this noble king
And wet his grave with my repentant tears,
I will with all expedient duty see you.
For divers unknown reasons, I beseech you,
Grant me this boon.

ANNE

With all my heart; and much it joys me too
220   To see you are become so penitent.
Tressel and Berkeley, go along with me.

RICHARD

Bid me farewell.

ANNE   'Tis more than you deserve;
But since you teach me how to flatter you,
Imagine I have said farewell already.

Exeunt Tressel and Berkeley, with Anne

RICHARD

Sirs, take up the corse.

GENTLEMAN   Towards Chertsey, noble lord?

RICHARD

No, to Whitefriars – there attend my coming.

Exeunt bearers and guard with corse

Was ever woman in this humour wooed?
Was ever woman in this humour won?
I'll have her, but I will not keep her long.
230   What? I that killed her husband and his father
To take her in her heart's extremest hate,

70

With curses in her mouth, tears in her eyes,
The bleeding witness of my hatred by,
Having God, her conscience, and these bars against me,
And I no friends to back my suit at all
But the plain devil and dissembling looks?
And yet to win her! All the world to nothing!
Ha!
Hath she forgot already that brave prince,
Edward, her lord, whom I, some three months since,   240
Stabbed in my angry mood at Tewkesbury?
A sweeter and a lovelier gentleman,
Framed in the prodigality of nature,
Young, valiant, wise, and, no doubt, right royal,
The spacious world cannot again afford;
And will she yet abase her eyes on me,
That cropped the golden prime of this sweet prince
And made her widow to a woeful bed?
On me, whose all not equals Edward's moiety?
On me, that halts and am misshapen thus?   250
My dukedom to a beggarly denier
I do mistake my person all this while!
Upon my life, she finds, although I cannot,
Myself to be a marvellous proper man.
I'll be at charges for a looking-glass
And entertain a score or two of tailors
To study fashions to adorn my body;
Since I am crept in favour with myself
I will maintain it with some little cost.
But first I'll turn yon fellow in his grave,   260
And then return lamenting to my love.
Shine out, fair sun, till I have bought a glass,
That I may see my shadow as I pass.   *Exit*

I.3   *Enter Queen Elizabeth, Lord Rivers, Marquess of Dorset, and Lord Grey*

RIVERS

Have patience, madam; there's no doubt his majesty
Will soon recover his accustomed health.

GREY

In that you brook it ill, it makes him worse;
Therefore for God's sake entertain good comfort
And cheer his grace with quick and merry eyes.

QUEEN ELIZABETH

If he were dead, what would betide on me?

GREY

No other harm but loss of such a lord.

QUEEN ELIZABETH

The loss of such a lord includes all harm.

GREY

The heavens have blessed you with a goodly son
10   To be your comforter when he is gone.

QUEEN ELIZABETH

Ah, he is young; and his minority
Is put unto the trust of Richard Gloucester,
A man that loves not me, nor none of you.

RIVERS

Is it concluded he shall be Protector?

QUEEN ELIZABETH

It is determined, not concluded yet;
But so it must be, if the King miscarry.
        Enter Buckingham and Derby

GREY

Here come the lords of Buckingham and Derby.

BUCKINGHAM

Good time of day unto your royal grace!

DERBY

God make your majesty joyful, as you have been!

QUEEN ELIZABETH
   The Countess Richmond, good my Lord of Derby,   20
   To your good prayer will scarcely say amen.
   Yet, Derby, notwithstanding she's your wife
   And loves not me, be you, good lord, assured
   I hate not you for her proud arrogance.

DERBY
   I do beseech you, either not believe
   The envious slanders of her false accusers;
   Or, if she be accused on true report,
   Bear with her weakness, which I think proceeds
   From wayward sickness, and no grounded malice.

QUEEN ELIZABETH
   Saw you the King today, my Lord of Derby?   30

DERBY
   But now the Duke of Buckingham and I
   Are come from visiting his majesty.

QUEEN ELIZABETH
   What likelihood of his amendment, lords?

BUCKINGHAM
   Madam, good hope; his grace speaks cheerfully.

QUEEN ELIZABETH
   God grant him health! Did you confer with him?

BUCKINGHAM
   Ay, madam; he desires to make atonement
   Between the Duke of Gloucester and your brothers,
   And between them and my Lord Chamberlain,
   And sent to warn them to his royal presence.

QUEEN ELIZABETH
   Would all were well! But that will never be.   40
   I fear our happiness is at the highest.
      Enter Richard, Duke of Gloucester, and Lord Hastings

RICHARD
   They do me wrong, and I will not endure it!

Who is it that complains unto the King
That I, forsooth, am stern, and love them not?
By holy Paul, they love his grace but lightly
That fill his ears with such dissentious rumours.
Because I cannot flatter and look fair,
Smile in men's faces, smooth, deceive, and cog,
Duck with French nods and apish courtesy,
50 I must be held a rancorous enemy.
Cannot a plain man live and think no harm,
But thus his simple truth must be abused
With silken, sly, insinuating Jacks?

GREY

To whom in all this presence speaks your grace?

RICHARD

To thee, that hast nor honesty nor grace.
When have I injured thee? When done thee wrong?
Or thee? Or thee? Or any of your faction?
A plague upon you all! His royal grace –
Whom God preserve better than you would wish! –
60 Cannot be quiet scarce a breathing while
But you must trouble him with lewd complaints.

QUEEN ELIZABETH

Brother of Gloucester, you mistake the matter.
The King, of his own royal disposition,
And not provoked by any suitor else,
Aiming, belike, at your interior hatred,
That in your outward action shows itself
Against my children, brothers, and myself,
Makes him to send, that he may learn the ground.

RICHARD

I cannot tell; the world is grown so bad
70 That wrens make prey where eagles dare not perch.
Since every Jack became a gentleman
There's many a gentle person made a Jack.

QUEEN ELIZABETH

Come, come, we know your meaning, brother
        Gloucester:
You envy my advancement and my friends'.
God grant we never may have need of you!

RICHARD

Meantime, God grants that I have need of you.
Our brother is imprisoned by your means,
Myself disgraced, and the nobility
Held in contempt, while great promotions
Are daily given to ennoble those   80
That scarce, some two days since, were worth a noble.

QUEEN ELIZABETH

By Him that raised me to this careful height
From that contented hap which I enjoyed,
I never did incense his majesty
Against the Duke of Clarence, but have been
An earnest advocate to plead for him.
My lord, you do me shameful injury
Falsely to draw me in these vile suspects.

RICHARD

You may deny that you were not the mean
Of my Lord Hastings' late imprisonment.   90

RIVERS

She may, my lord, for –

RICHARD

She may, Lord Rivers! Why, who knows not so?
She may do more, sir, than denying that;
She may help you to many fair preferments,
And then deny her aiding hand therein
And lay those honours on your high desert.
What may she not? She may, yea, marry, may she –

RIVERS

What, marry, may she?

75

RICHARD

> What, marry, may she? Marry with a king,
> A bachelor and a handsome stripling too!
> Iwis your grandam had a worser match.

QUEEN ELIZABETH

> My Lord of Gloucester, I have too long borne
> Your blunt upbraidings and your bitter scoffs.
> By heaven, I will acquaint his majesty
> Of those gross taunts that oft I have endured.
> I had rather be a country servant-maid
> Than a great queen, with this condition,
> To be so baited, scorned, and stormèd at;
> > *Enter old Queen Margaret, behind*
> Small joy have I in being England's Queen.

QUEEN MARGARET (*aside*)

> And lessened be that small, God I beseech Him!
> Thy honour, state, and seat is due to me.

RICHARD

> What? Threat you me with telling of the King?
> Tell him, and spare not. Look what I have said
> I will avouch't in presence of the King;
> I dare adventure to be sent to the Tower.
> 'Tis time to speak, my pains are quite forgot.

QUEEN MARGARET (*aside*)

> Out, devil! I do remember them too well.
> Thou kill'dst my husband Henry in the Tower,
> And Edward, my poor son, at Tewkesbury.

RICHARD

> Ere you were queen, yea, or your husband king,
> I was a packhorse in his great affairs;
> A weeder-out of his proud adversaries,
> A liberal rewarder of his friends.
> To royalize his blood I spent mine own.

QUEEN MARGARET (*aside*)

Yea, and much better blood than his or thine.

RICHARD

In all which time you and your husband Grey
Were factious for the house of Lancaster;
And, Rivers, so were you. Was not your husband
In Margaret's battle at Saint Albans slain?
Let me put in your minds, if you forget,   130
What you have been ere this, and what you are;
Withal, what I have been, and what I am.

QUEEN MARGARET (*aside*)

A murderous villain, and so still thou art.

RICHARD

Poor Clarence did forsake his father, Warwick;
Yea, and forswore himself, which Jesu pardon! –

QUEEN MARGARET (*aside*)

Which God revenge!

RICHARD

– To fight on Edward's party for the crown;
And for his meed, poor lord, he is mewed up.
I would to God my heart were flint like Edward's,
Or Edward's soft and pitiful like mine!   140
I am too childish-foolish for this world.

QUEEN MARGARET (*aside*)

Hie thee to hell for shame, and leave this world,
Thou cacodemon! There thy kingdom is.

RIVERS

My Lord of Gloucester, in those busy days
Which here you urge to prove us enemies,
We followed then our lord, our sovereign king;
So should we you, if you should be our king.

RICHARD

If I should be? I had rather be a pedlar.
Far be it from my heart, the thought thereof!

QUEEN ELIZABETH

150   As little joy, my lord, as you suppose
You should enjoy, were you this country's king,
As little joy you may suppose in me
That I enjoy, being the Queen thereof.

QUEEN MARGARET (*aside*)

As little joy enjoys the Queen thereof;
For I am she, and altogether joyless.
I can no longer hold me patient.
She comes forward
Hear me, you wrangling pirates, that fall out
In sharing that which you have pilled from me!
Which of you trembles not that looks on me?

160   If not, that I am Queen, you bow like subjects,
Yet that, by you deposed, you quake like rebels?
Ah, gentle villain, do not turn away!

RICHARD

Foul wrinkled witch, what mak'st thou in my sight?

QUEEN MARGARET

But repetition of what thou hast marred,
That will I make before I let thee go.

RICHARD

Wert thou not banishèd on pain of death?

QUEEN MARGARET

I was; but I do find more pain in banishment
Than death can yield me here by my abode.
A husband and a son thou ow'st to me –

170   And thou a kingdom – all of you allegiance.
This sorrow that I have, by right is yours,
And all the pleasures you usurp are mine.

RICHARD

The curse my noble father laid on thee
When thou didst crown his warlike brows with paper
And with thy scorns drew'st rivers from his eyes,

And then, to dry them, gav'st the Duke a clout
Steeped in the faultless blood of pretty Rutland –
His curses then, from bitterness of soul
Denounced against thee, are all fallen upon thee;
And God, not we, hath plagued thy bloody deed. 180

QUEEN ELIZABETH
So just is God, to right the innocent.

HASTINGS
O, 'twas the foulest deed to slay that babe,
And the most merciless, that e'er was heard of!

RIVERS
Tyrants themselves wept when it was reported.

DORSET
No man but prophesied revenge for it.

BUCKINGHAM
Northumberland, then present, wept to see it.

QUEEN MARGARET
What! Were you snarling all before I came,
Ready to catch each other by the throat,
And turn you all your hatred now on me?
Did York's dread curse prevail so much with heaven 190
That Henry's death, my lovely Edward's death,
Their kingdom's loss, my woeful banishment,
Should all but answer for that peevish brat?
Can curses pierce the clouds and enter heaven?
Why then, give way, dull clouds, to my quick curses!
Though not by war, by surfeit die your king,
As ours by murder, to make him a king!
Edward thy son, that now is Prince of Wales,
For Edward our son, that was Prince of Wales,
Die in his youth by like untimely violence! 200
Thyself a queen, for me that was a queen,
Outlive thy glory, like my wretched self!
Long mayst thou live to wail thy children's death

And see another, as I see thee now,
Decked in thy rights as thou art stalled in mine!
Long die thy happy days before thy death,
And after many lengthened hours of grief,
Die neither mother, wife, nor England's queen!
Rivers and Dorset, you were standers-by,
And so wast thou, Lord Hastings, when my son
Was stabbed with bloody daggers. God, I pray Him,
That none of you may live his natural age,
But by some unlooked accident cut off!

RICHARD
Have done thy charm, thou hateful withered hag!

QUEEN MARGARET
And leave out thee? Stay, dog, for thou shalt hear me.
If heaven have any grievous plague in store
Exceeding those that I can wish upon thee,
O let them keep it till thy sins be ripe,
And then hurl down their indignation
On thee, the troubler of the poor world's peace!
The worm of conscience still begnaw thy soul!
Thy friends suspect for traitors while thou liv'st,
And take deep traitors for thy dearest friends!
No sleep close up that deadly eye of thine,
Unless it be while some tormenting dream
Affrights thee with a hell of ugly devils!
Thou elvish-marked, abortive, rooting hog!
Thou that wast sealed in thy nativity
The slave of nature and the son of hell!
Thou slander of thy heavy mother's womb!
Thou loathèd issue of thy father's loins!
Thou rag of honour! Thou detested –

RICHARD
Margaret.

QUEEN MARGARET Richard!

RICHARD   Ha?

QUEEN MARGARET   I call thee not.

RICHARD

  I cry thee mercy then; for I did think

  That thou hadst called me all these bitter names.

QUEEN MARGARET

  Why, so I did, but looked for no reply.

  O, let me make the period to my curse!

RICHARD

  'Tis done by me, and ends in 'Margaret'.

QUEEN ELIZABETH

  Thus have you breathed your curse against yourself.

QUEEN MARGARET

  Poor painted queen, vain flourish of my fortune!   240

  Why strew'st thou sugar on that bottled spider

  Whose deadly web ensnareth thee about?

  Fool, fool! Thou whet'st a knife to kill thyself.

  The day will come that thou shalt wish for me

  To help thee curse this poisonous bunch-backed toad.

HASTINGS

  False-boding woman, end thy frantic curse,

  Lest to thy harm thou move our patience.

QUEEN MARGARET

  Foul shame upon you! You have all moved mine.

RIVERS

  Were you well served, you would be taught your duty.

QUEEN MARGARET

  To serve me well, you all should do me duty,   250

  Teach me to be your queen, and you my subjects.

  O, serve me well, and teach yourselves that duty!

DORSET

  Dispute not with her; she is lunatic.

QUEEN MARGARET

  Peace, master Marquess, you are malapert.

Your fire-new stamp of honour is scarce current.
O, that your young nobility could judge
What 'twere to lose it and be miserable!
They that stand high have many blasts to shake them,
And if they fall, they dash themselves to pieces.

RICHARD

260 Good counsel, marry! Learn it, learn it, Marquess.

DORSET

It touches you, my lord, as much as me.

RICHARD

Yea, and much more; but I was born so high.
Our aery buildeth in the cedar's top
And dallies with the wind and scorns the sun.

QUEEN MARGARET

And turns the sun to shade – alas! alas!
Witness my son, now in the shade of death,
Whose bright outshining beams thy cloudy wrath
Hath in eternal darkness folded up.
Your aery buildeth in our aery's nest.

270 O God, that seest it, do not suffer it!
As it is won with blood, lost be it so!

BUCKINGHAM

Peace, peace, for shame, if not for charity.

QUEEN MARGARET

Urge neither charity nor shame to me.
Uncharitably with me have you dealt,
And shamefully my hopes by you are butchered.
My charity is outrage, life my shame,
And in that shame still live my sorrow's rage!

BUCKINGHAM

Have done, have done.

QUEEN MARGARET

O princely Buckingham, I'll kiss thy hand
280 In sign of league and amity with thee.

Now fair befall thee and thy noble house!
Thy garments are not spotted with our blood,
Nor thou within the compass of my curse.

BUCKINGHAM

Nor no one here; for curses never pass
The lips of those that breathe them in the air.

QUEEN MARGARET

I will not think but they ascend the sky
And there awake God's gentle-sleeping peace.
O Buckingham, take heed of yonder dog!
Look when he fawns he bites; and when he bites
His venom tooth will rankle to the death.   290
Have not to do with him, beware of him.
Sin, death, and hell have set their marks on him,
And all their ministers attend on him.

RICHARD

What doth she say, my Lord of Buckingham?

BUCKINGHAM

Nothing that I respect, my gracious lord.

QUEEN MARGARET

What, dost thou scorn me for my gentle counsel?
And soothe the devil that I warn thee from?
O, but remember this another day,
When he shall split thy very heart with sorrow,
And say poor Margaret was a prophetess!   300
Live each of you the subjects to his hate,
And he to yours, and all of you to God's!   *Exit*

BUCKINGHAM

My hair doth stand an end to hear her curses.

RIVERS

And so doth mine. I muse why she's at liberty.

RICHARD

I cannot blame her. By God's holy Mother,
She hath had too much wrong, and I repent

My part thereof that I have done to her.

QUEEN ELIZABETH

I never did her any, to my knowledge.

RICHARD

Yet you have all the vantage of her wrong.

310 – I was too hot to do somebody good
That is too cold in thinking of it now.
Marry, as for Clarence, he is well repaid;
He is franked up to fatting for his pains –
God pardon them that are the cause thereof!

RIVERS

A virtuous and a Christian-like conclusion –
To pray for them that have done scathe to us.

RICHARD

So do I ever – (*aside*) being well advised;
For had I cursed now, I had cursed myself.
Enter Catesby

CATESBY

Madam, his majesty doth call for you;

320 And for your grace; and yours, my gracious lord.

QUEEN ELIZABETH

Catesby, I come. Lords, will you go with me?

RIVERS

We wait upon your grace.
Exeunt all but Richard, Duke of Gloucester

RICHARD

I do the wrong, and first begin to brawl.
The secret mischiefs that I set abroach
I lay unto the grievous charge of others.
Clarence, whom I indeed have cast in darkness,
I do beweep to many simple gulls –
Namely, to Derby, Hastings, Buckingham –
And tell them 'tis the Queen and her allies

330 That stir the King against the Duke my brother.

Now they believe it, and withal whet me
To be revenged on Rivers, Dorset, Grey.
But then I sigh, and, with a piece of Scripture,
Tell them that God bids us do good for evil;
And thus I clothe my naked villainy
With odd old ends stolen forth of Holy Writ,
And seem a saint, when most I play the devil.

Enter two Murderers

But soft! Here come my executioners.
How now, my hardy, stout, resolvèd mates!
Are you now going to dispatch this thing?   340

FIRST MURDERER

We are, my lord, and come to have the warrant,
That we may be admitted where he is.

RICHARD

Well thought upon; I have it here about me.
He gives the warrant
When you have done, repair to Crosby Place.
But, sirs, be sudden in the execution,
Withal obdurate, do not hear him plead;
For Clarence is well-spoken, and perhaps
May move your hearts to pity if you mark him.

FIRST MURDERER

Tut, tut, my lord! We will not stand to prate;
Talkers are no good doers. Be assured: 350
We go to use our hands, and not our tongues.

RICHARD

Your eyes drop millstones when fools' eyes fall tears.
I like you, lads; about your business straight.
Go, go, dispatch.

FIRST MURDERER We will, my noble lord.   *Exeunt*

KEEPER

Why looks your grace so heavily today?

CLARENCE

O, I have passed a miserable night,
So full of fearful dreams, of ugly sights,
That, as I am a Christian faithful man,
I would not spend another such a night
Though 'twere to buy a world of happy days,
So full of dismal terror was the time.

KEEPER

What was your dream, my lord? I pray you tell me.

CLARENCE

Methoughts that I had broken from the Tower
10 And was embarked to cross to Burgundy,
And in my company my brother Gloucester,
Who from my cabin tempted me to walk
Upon the hatches; thence we looked toward England
And cited up a thousand heavy times,
During the wars of York and Lancaster,
That had befallen us. As we paced along
Upon the giddy footing of the hatches,
Methought that Gloucester stumbled, and in falling
Struck me, that thought to stay him, overboard
20 Into the tumbling billows of the main.
O Lord! Methought what pain it was to drown!
What dreadful noise of waters in mine ears!
What sights of ugly death within mine eyes!
Methoughts I saw a thousand fearful wracks;
A thousand men that fishes gnawed upon;
Wedges of gold, great anchors, heaps of pearl,
Inestimable stones, unvalued jewels,
All scattered in the bottom of the sea.
Some lay in dead men's skulls, and in the holes

Where eyes did once inhabit, there were crept,
As 'twere in scorn of eyes, reflecting gems,
That wooed the slimy bottom of the deep
And mocked the dead bones that lay scattered by.

KEEPER

Had you such leisure in the time of death,
To gaze upon these secrets of the deep?

CLARENCE

Methought I had; and often did I strive
To yield the ghost; but still the envious flood
Stopped in my soul, and would not let it forth
To find the empty, vast, and wandering air,
But smothered it within my panting bulk,
Who almost burst to belch it in the sea.

KEEPER

Awaked you not in this sore agony?

CLARENCE

No, no, my dream was lengthened after life.
O then began the tempest to my soul!
I passed, methought, the melancholy flood,
With that sour ferryman which poets write of,
Unto the kingdom of perpetual night.
The first that there did greet my stranger soul
Was my great father-in-law, renownèd Warwick,
Who spake aloud, 'What scourge for perjury
Can this dark monarchy afford false Clarence?'
And so he vanished. Then came wandering by
A shadow like an angel, with bright hair
Dabbled in blood, and he shrieked out aloud,
'Clarence is come – false, fleeting, perjured Clarence,
That stabbed me in the field by Tewkesbury.
Seize on him, Furies, take him unto torment!'
With that, methoughts, a legion of foul fiends
Environed me, and howlèd in mine ears

60   Such hideous cries that with the very noise
     I, trembling, waked, and for a season after
     Could not believe but that I was in hell,
     Such terrible impression made my dream.

KEEPER

     No marvel, my lord, though it affrighted you;
     I am afraid, methinks, to hear you tell it.

CLARENCE

     Ah, keeper, keeper, I have done these things,
     That now give evidence against my soul,
     For Edward's sake, and see how he requits me!
     O God! If my deep prayers cannot appease Thee,
70   But Thou wilt be avenged on my misdeeds,
     Yet execute Thy wrath in me alone;
     O, spare my guiltless wife and my poor children!
     Keeper, I pray thee, sit by me awhile.
     My soul is heavy, and I fain would sleep.

KEEPER

     I will, my lord. God give your grace good rest!
             Clarence sleeps
             Enter Brakenbury, the Lieutenant

BRAKENBURY

     Sorrow breaks seasons and reposing hours,
     Makes the night morning and the noontide night.
     Princes have but their titles for their glories,
     An outward honour for an inward toil;
80   And for unfelt imaginations
     They often feel a world of restless cares;
     So that between their titles and low name
     There's nothing differs but the outward fame.
             Enter two Murderers

FIRST MURDERER Ho! Who's here?

BRAKENBURY What wouldst thou, fellow? And how
     cam'st thou hither?

88

SECOND MURDERER I would speak with Clarence, and I
came hither on my legs.

BRAKENBURY Yea, so brief?

FIRST MURDERER 'Tis better, sir, than to be tedious. 90
Let him see our commission, and talk no more.

Brakenbury reads it

BRAKENBURY
I am in this commanded to deliver
The noble Duke of Clarence to your hands.
I will not reason what is meant hereby,
Because I will be guiltless from the meaning.
There lies the Duke asleep, and there the keys.
I'll to the King, and signify to him
That thus I have resigned to you my charge.

Exit Brakenbury with Keeper

FIRST MURDERER You may, sir; 'tis a point of wisdom.
Fare you well. 100

SECOND MURDERER What? Shall I stab him as he sleeps?

FIRST MURDERER No. He'll say 'twas done cowardly
when he wakes.

SECOND MURDERER Why, he shall never wake until the
great Judgement Day.

FIRST MURDERER Why, then he'll say we stabbed him
sleeping.

SECOND MURDERER The urging of that word judgement
hath bred a kind of remorse in me.

FIRST MURDERER What? Art thou afraid? 110

SECOND MURDERER Not to kill him, having a warrant,
but to be damned for killing him, from the which no
warrant can defend me.

FIRST MURDERER I thought thou hadst been resolute.

SECOND MURDERER So I am – to let him live.

FIRST MURDERER I'll back to the Duke of Gloucester
and tell him so.

SECOND MURDERER Nay, I pray thee stay a little. I hope
this passionate humour of mine will change. It was wont
120 to hold me but while one tells twenty.

FIRST MURDERER How dost thou feel thyself now?

SECOND MURDERER Faith, some certain dregs of conscience are yet within me.

FIRST MURDERER Remember our reward when the
deed's done.

SECOND MURDERER Zounds, he dies! I had forgot the
reward.

FIRST MURDERER Where's thy conscience now?

SECOND MURDERER O, in the Duke of Gloucester's
130 purse.

FIRST MURDERER When he opens his purse to give us
our reward, thy conscience flies out.

SECOND MURDERER 'Tis no matter; let it go. There's
few or none will entertain it.

FIRST MURDERER What if it come to thee again?

SECOND MURDERER I'll not meddle with it; it makes a
man a coward. A man cannot steal, but it accuseth him;
a man cannot swear, but it checks him; a man cannot lie
with his neighbour's wife, but it detects him. 'Tis a
140 blushing shamefaced spirit that mutinies in a man's
bosom. It fills a man full of obstacles. It made me once
restore a purse of gold that by chance I found. It beggars
any man that keeps it. It is turned out of towns and
cities for a dangerous thing, and every man that means
to live well endeavours to trust to himself and live without it.

FIRST MURDERER Zounds, 'tis even now at my elbow,
persuading me not to kill the Duke.

SECOND MURDERER Take the devil in thy mind – and
150 believe him not. He would insinuate with thee but to
make thee sigh.

FIRST MURDERER Tut, I am strong-framed; he cannot prevail with me.

SECOND MURDERER Spoke like a tall man that respects thy reputation. Come, shall we fall to work?

FIRST MURDERER Take him on the costard with the hilts of thy sword, and then throw him into the malmsey-butt in the next room.

SECOND MURDERER O excellent device! And make a sop of him.   160

FIRST MURDERER Soft! He wakes.

SECOND MURDERER Strike!

FIRST MURDERER No, we'll reason with him.

CLARENCE

Where art thou, keeper? Give me a cup of wine.

SECOND MURDERER

You shall have wine enough, my lord, anon.

CLARENCE

In God's name, what art thou?

FIRST MURDERER A man, as you are.

CLARENCE But not as I am, royal.

SECOND MURDERER Nor you as we are, loyal.

CLARENCE

Thy voice is thunder, but thy looks are humble.   170

FIRST MURDERER

My voice is now the King's, my looks mine own.

CLARENCE

How darkly and how deadly dost thou speak!
Your eyes do menace me. Why look you pale?
Who sent you hither? Wherefore do you come?

SECOND MURDERER To, to, to –

CLARENCE To murder me?

FIRST and SECOND MURDERER Ay, ay.

CLARENCE

You scarcely have the hearts to tell me so,

And therefore cannot have the hearts to do it.
180 Wherein, my friends, have I offended you?

FIRST MURDERER
Offended us you have not, but the King.

CLARENCE
I shall be reconciled to him again.

SECOND MURDERER
Never, my lord; therefore prepare to die.

CLARENCE
Are you drawn forth among a world of men
To slay the innocent? What is my offence?
Where is the evidence that doth accuse me?
What lawful quest have given their verdict up
Unto the frowning judge? Or who pronounced
The bitter sentence of poor Clarence' death
190 Before I be convict by course of law?
To threaten me with death is most unlawful.
I charge you, as you hope to have redemption
By Christ's dear blood shed for our grievous sins,
That you depart, and lay no hands on me.
The deed you undertake is damnable.

FIRST MURDERER
What we will do, we do upon command.

SECOND MURDERER
And he that hath commanded is our king.

CLARENCE
Erroneous vassals! The great King of kings
Hath in the table of His law commanded
200 That thou shalt do no murder. Will you then
Spurn at His edict, and fulfil a man's?
Take heed; for He holds vengeance in His hand
To hurl upon their heads that break His law.

SECOND MURDERER
And that same vengeance doth He hurl on thee

For false forswearing and for murder too:
Thou didst receive the sacrament to fight
In quarrel of the house of Lancaster.

FIRST MURDERER

And like a traitor to the name of God
Didst break that vow, and with thy treacherous blade
Unrip'st the bowels of thy sovereign's son.   210

SECOND MURDERER

Whom thou wast sworn to cherish and defend.

FIRST MURDERER

How canst thou urge God's dreadful law to us
When thou hast broke it in such dear degree?

CLARENCE

Alas! For whose sake did I that ill deed?
For Edward, for my brother, for his sake.
He sends you not to murder me for this,
For in that sin he is as deep as I.
If God will be avengèd for the deed,
O, know you yet He doth it publicly!
Take not the quarrel from His powerful arm.   220
He needs no indirect or lawless course
To cut off those that have offended Him.

FIRST MURDERER

Who made thee then a bloody minister
When gallant-springing brave Plantagenet,
That princely novice, was struck dead by thee?

CLARENCE

My brother's love, the devil, and my rage.

FIRST MURDERER

Thy brother's love, our duty, and thy fault
Provoke us hither now to slaughter thee.

CLARENCE

If you do love my brother, hate not me;
I am his brother, and I love him well.   230

If you are hired for meed, go back again,
And I will send you to my brother Gloucester,
Who shall reward you better for my life
Than Edward will for tidings of my death.

SECOND MURDERER
You are deceived. Your brother Gloucester hates you.

CLARENCE
O, no, he loves me and he holds me dear!
Go you to him from me.

FIRST MURDERER   Ay, so we will.

CLARENCE
Tell him, when that our princely father York
Blessed his three sons with his victorious arm
240 And charged us from his soul to love each other,
He little thought of this divided friendship;
Bid Gloucester think of this, and he will weep.

FIRST MURDERER
Ay, millstones, as he lessoned us to weep.

CLARENCE
O, do not slander him, for he is kind.

FIRST MURDERER
Right, as snow in harvest. Come, you deceive yourself;
'Tis he that sends us to destroy you here.

CLARENCE
It cannot be, for he bewept my fortune,
And hugged me in his arms, and swore with sobs
That he would labour my delivery.

FIRST MURDERER
250 Why, so he doth, when he delivers you
From this earth's thraldom to the joys of heaven.

SECOND MURDERER
Make peace with God, for you must die, my lord.

CLARENCE
Have you that holy feeling in your souls

To counsel me to make my peace with God,
And are you yet to your own souls so blind
That you will war with God by murdering me?
O, sirs, consider, they that set you on
To do this deed will hate you for the deed.

SECOND MURDERER
What shall we do?

CLARENCE   Relent, and save your souls.
Which of you, if you were a prince's son,   260
Being pent from liberty, as I am now,
If two such murderers as yourselves came to you,
Would not entreat for life? As you would beg
Were you in my distress –

FIRST MURDERER
Relent? No: 'tis cowardly and womanish.

CLARENCE
Not to relent is beastly, savage, devilish!
(*To Second Murderer*)
My friend, I spy some pity in thy looks.
O, if thine eye be not a flatterer,
Come thou on my side, and entreat for me!
A begging prince what beggar pities not?   270

SECOND MURDERER Look behind you, my lord!

FIRST MURDERER
Take that! And that! (*Stabs him*) If all this will not do,
I'll drown you in the malmsey-butt within.
         Exit with the body

SECOND MURDERER
A bloody deed, and desperately dispatched!
How fain, like Pilate, would I wash my hands
Of this most grievous murder!
  Enter First Murderer

FIRST MURDERER
How now? What mean'st thou that thou help'st me not?

By heavens, the Duke shall know how slack you have
been.

SECOND MURDERER

I would he knew that I had saved his brother!

280 Take thou the fee and tell him what I say,

For I repent me that the Duke is slain. *Exit*

FIRST MURDERER

So do not I. Go, coward as thou art.

Well, I'll go hide the body in some hole

Till that the Duke give order for his burial;

And when I have my meed, I will away,

For this will out, and then I must not stay. *Exit*

✳

II.1   *Flourish. Enter King Edward, sick, the Queen, Lord*
Marquess Dorset, Grey, Rivers, Hastings, Catesby,
Buckingham, and attendants

KING EDWARD

Why, so; now have I done a good day's work.

You peers, continue this united league.

I every day expect an embassage

From my Redeemer to redeem me hence;

And more in peace my soul shall part to heaven,

Since I have made my friends at peace on earth.

Hastings and Rivers, take each other's hand;

Dissemble not your hatred, swear your love.

RIVERS

By heaven, my soul is purged from grudging hate,

10 And with my hand I seal my true heart's love.

HASTINGS

So thrive I as I truly swear the like!

KING EDWARD

Take heed you dally not before your King,

Lest He that is the supreme King of kings
Confound your hidden falsehood and award
Either of you to be the other's end.

HASTINGS
So prosper I as I swear perfect love!

RIVERS
And I as I love Hastings with my heart!

KING EDWARD
Madam, yourself is not exempt from this;
Nor you, son Dorset; Buckingham, nor you.
You have been factious one against the other.   20
Wife, love Lord Hastings, let him kiss your hand,
And what you do, do it unfeignedly.

QUEEN ELIZABETH
There, Hastings, I will never more remember
Our former hatred, so thrive I and mine!

KING EDWARD
Dorset, embrace him; Hastings, love Lord Marquess.

DORSET
This interchange of love, I here protest,
Upon my part shall be inviolable.

HASTINGS
And so swear I.

KING EDWARD
Now, princely Buckingham, seal thou this league
With thy embracements to my wife's allies,   30
And make me happy in your unity.

BUCKINGHAM (to the Queen)
Whenever Buckingham doth turn his hate
Upon your grace, but with all duteous love
Doth cherish you and yours, God punish me
With hate in those where I expect most love!
When I have most need to employ a friend,
And most assurèd that he is a friend,

Deep, hollow, treacherous, and full of guile
Be he unto me! This do I beg of God,
40   When I am cold in love to you or yours.
      Embrace

KING EDWARD

A pleasing cordial, princely Buckingham,
Is this thy vow unto my sickly heart.
There wanteth now our brother Gloucester here
To make the blessèd period of this peace.

BUCKINGHAM

And, in good time,
Here comes Sir Richard Ratcliffe and the Duke.
      Enter Sir Richard Ratcliffe and Richard, Duke of
      Gloucester

RICHARD

Good morrow to my sovereign King and Queen;
And, princely peers, a happy time of day!

KING EDWARD

Happy indeed, as we have spent the day.
50   Gloucester, we have done deeds of charity,
Made peace of enmity, fair love of hate,
Between these swelling, wrong-incensèd peers.

RICHARD

A blessèd labour, my most sovereign lord.
Among this princely heap, if any here
By false intelligence or wrong surmise
Hold me a foe –
If I unwittingly, or in my rage,
Have aught committed that is hardly borne
By any in this presence, I desire
60   To reconcile me to his friendly peace.
'Tis death to me to be at enmity;
I hate it, and desire all good men's love.
First, madam, I entreat true peace of you,

Which I will purchase with my duteous service;
Of you, my noble cousin Buckingham,
If ever any grudge were lodged between us;
Of you, and you, Lord Rivers, and of Dorset,
That, all without desert, have frowned on me;
Of you, Lord Woodville, and, Lord Scales, of you;
Dukes, earls, lords, gentlemen – indeed, of all.   70
I do not know that Englishman alive
With whom my soul is any jot at odds
More than the infant that is born tonight.
I thank my God for my humility!

QUEEN ELIZABETH

A holy day shall this be kept hereafter;
I would to God all strifes were well compounded.
My sovereign lord, I do beseech your highness
To take our brother Clarence to your grace.

RICHARD

Why, madam, have I offered love for this,
To be so flouted in this royal presence?   80
Who knows not that the gentle Duke is dead?
        They all start
You do him injury to scorn his corse.

KING EDWARD

Who knows not he is dead? Who knows he is?

QUEEN ELIZABETH

All-seeing heaven, what a world is this!

BUCKINGHAM

Look I so pale, Lord Dorset, as the rest?

DORSET

Ay, my good lord; and no man in the presence
But his red colour hath forsook his cheeks.

KING EDWARD

Is Clarence dead? The order was reversed.

RICHARD

> But he, poor man, by your first order died,
90 > And that a wingèd Mercury did bear.
> Some tardy cripple bare the countermand,
> That came too lag to see him buried.
> God grant that some, less noble and less loyal,
> Nearer in bloody thoughts, but not in blood,
> Deserve not worse than wretched Clarence did,
> And yet go current from suspicion!

Enter the Earl of Derby

DERBY

> A boon, my sovereign, for my service done!

KING EDWARD

> I pray thee peace. My soul is full of sorrow.

DERBY

> I will not rise unless your highness hear me.

KING EDWARD

100 > Then say at once what is it thou requests.

DERBY

> The forfeit, sovereign, of my servant's life,
> Who slew today a riotous gentleman
> Lately attendant on the Duke of Norfolk.

KING EDWARD

> Have I a tongue to doom my brother's death,
> And shall that tongue give pardon to a slave?
> My brother killed no man – his fault was thought –
> And yet his punishment was bitter death.
> Who sued to me for him? Who, in my wrath,
> Kneeled at my feet and bid me be advised?
110 > Who spoke of brotherhood? Who spoke of love?
> Who told me how the poor soul did forsake
> The mighty Warwick and did fight for me?
> Who told me, in the field at Tewkesbury,
> When Oxford had me down, he rescued me

And said, 'Dear brother, live, and be a king'?
Who told me, when we both lay in the field
Frozen almost to death, how he did lap me
Even in his garments, and did give himself,
All thin and naked, to the numb-cold night?
All this from my remembrance brutish wrath   120
Sinfully plucked, and not a man of you
Had so much grace to put it in my mind.
But when your carters or your waiting vassals
Have done a drunken slaughter and defaced
The precious image of our dear Redeemer,
You straight are on your knees for pardon, pardon;
And I, unjustly too, must grant it you.
    Derby rises
But for my brother not a man would speak,
Nor I, ungracious, speak unto myself
For him, poor soul! The proudest of you all   130
Have been beholding to him in his life;
Yet none of you would once beg for his life.
O God! I fear thy justice will take hold
On me and you, and mine and yours, for this.
Come, Hastings, help me to my closet. Ah, poor
      Clarence!   *Exeunt some with King and Queen*

RICHARD
This is the fruits of rashness! Marked you not
How that the guilty kindred of the Queen
Looked pale when they did hear of Clarence' death?
O, they did urge it still unto the King!
God will revenge it. Come, lords, will you go   140
To comfort Edward with our company?

BUCKINGHAM
We wait upon your grace.   *Exeunt*

Enter the old Duchess of York, with Edward and
                Margaret Plantagenet (the two children of Clarence)

BOY
    Good grandam, tell us, is our father dead?

DUCHESS OF YORK
    No, boy.

GIRL
    Why do you weep so oft, and beat your breast,
    And cry 'O Clarence, my unhappy son'?

BOY
    Why do you look on us, and shake your head,
    And call us orphans, wretches, castaways,
    If that our noble father were alive?

DUCHESS OF YORK
    My pretty cousins, you mistake me both.
    I do lament the sickness of the King,
10   As loath to lose him, not your father's death;
    It were lost sorrow to wail one that's lost.

BOY
    Then you conclude, my grandam, he is dead?
    The King mine uncle is to blame for it.
    God will revenge it, whom I will importune
    With earnest prayers all to that effect.

GIRL
    And so will I.

DUCHESS OF YORK
    Peace, children, peace! The King doth love you well.
    Incapable and shallow innocents,
    You cannot guess who caused your father's death.

BOY
20   Grandam, we can; for my good uncle Gloucester
    Told me the King, provoked to it by the Queen,
    Devised impeachments to imprison him;
    And when my uncle told me so, he wept,

And pitied me, and kindly kissed my cheek;
Bade me rely on him as on my father,
And he would love me dearly as a child.

DUCHESS OF YORK

Ah, that deceit should steal such gentle shape
And with a virtuous visor hide deep vice!
He is my son – yea, and therein my shame;
Yet from my dugs he drew not this deceit.   30

BOY

Think you my uncle did dissemble, grandam?

DUCHESS OF YORK

Ay, boy.

BOY

I cannot think it. Hark! What noise is this?

Enter Queen Elizabeth, with her hair about her ears,
Rivers and Dorset after her

QUEEN ELIZABETH

Ah, who shall hinder me to wail and weep,
To chide my fortune, and torment myself?
I'll join with black despair against my soul
And to myself become an enemy.

DUCHESS OF YORK

What means this scene of rude impatience?

QUEEN ELIZABETH

To make an act of tragic violence.
Edward, my lord, thy son, our King, is dead!   40
Why grow the branches when the root is gone?
Why wither not the leaves that want their sap?
If you will live, lament; if die, be brief,
That our swift-wingèd souls may catch the King's,
Or like obedient subjects follow him
To his new kingdom of ne'er-changing night.

DUCHESS OF YORK

Ah, so much interest have I in thy sorrow

As I had title in thy noble husband.
I have bewept a worthy husband's death,
50 And lived with looking on his images;
But now two mirrors of his princely semblance
Are cracked in pieces by malignant death,
And I for comfort have but one false glass
That grieves me when I see my shame in him.
Thou art a widow; yet thou art a mother,
And hast the comfort of thy children left;
But death hath snatched my husband from mine arms
And plucked two crutches from my feeble hands,
Clarence and Edward. O, what cause have I,
60 Thine being but a moiety of my moan,
To overgo thy woes and drown thy cries!

BOY

Ah, aunt! You wept not for our father's death.
How can we aid you with our kindred tears?

GIRL

Our fatherless distress was left unmoaned:
Your widow-dolour likewise be unwept!

QUEEN ELIZABETH

Give me no help in lamentation;
I am not barren to bring forth complaints.
All springs reduce their currents to mine eyes,
That I, being governed by the watery moon,
70 May send forth plenteous tears to drown the world.
Ah for my husband, for my dear lord Edward!

CHILDREN

Ah for our father, for our dear lord Clarence!

DUCHESS OF YORK

Alas for both, both mine, Edward and Clarence!

QUEEN ELIZABETH

What stay had I but Edward? And he's gone.

CHILDREN

What stay had we but Clarence? And he's gone.

DUCHESS OF YORK

What stays had I but they? And they are gone.

QUEEN ELIZABETH

Was never widow had so dear a loss.

CHILDREN

Were never orphans had so dear a loss.

DUCHESS OF YORK

Was never mother had so dear a loss.
Alas! I am the mother of these griefs;   80
Their woes are parcelled, mine is general.
She for an Edward weeps, and so do I;
I for a Clarence weep, so doth not she;
These babes for Clarence weep, and so do I;
I for an Edward weep, so do not they.
Alas, you three on me, threefold distressed,
Pour all your tears! I am your sorrow's nurse,
And I will pamper it with lamentation.

DORSET

Comfort, dear mother; God is much displeased
That you take with unthankfulness His doing.   90
In common worldly things 'tis called ungrateful
With dull unwillingness to repay a debt
Which with a bounteous hand was kindly lent;
Much more to be thus opposite with heaven
For it requires the royal debt it lent you.

RIVERS

Madam, bethink you like a careful mother
Of the young prince, your son. Send straight for him,
Let him be crowned; in him your comfort lives.
Drown desperate sorrow in dead Edward's grave
And plant your joys in living Edward's throne.   100

Enter Richard, Duke of Gloucester, Buckingham,
Derby, Hastings, and Ratcliffe

RICHARD

  Sister, have comfort. All of us have cause
  To wail the dimming of our shining star;
  But none can help our harms by wailing them.
  Madam, my mother, I do cry you mercy;
  I did not see your grace. Humbly on my knee
  I crave your blessing.

DUCHESS OF YORK

  God bless thee, and put meekness in thy breast,
  Love, charity, obedience, and true duty!

RICHARD

  Amen! (*Aside*) And make me die a good old man!
110 That is the butt-end of a mother's blessing;
  I marvel that her grace did leave it out.

BUCKINGHAM

  You cloudy princes and heart-sorrowing peers
  That bear this heavy mutual load of moan,
  Now cheer each other in each other's love.
  Though we have spent our harvest of this king,
  We are to reap the harvest of his son.
  The broken rancour of your high-swollen hearts,
  But lately splintered, knit, and joined together,
  Must gently be preserved, cherished, and kept.
120 Me seemeth good that with some little train
  Forthwith from Ludlow the young Prince be fet
  Hither to London, to be crowned our King.

RIVERS

  Why with some little train, my Lord of Buckingham?

BUCKINGHAM

  Marry, my lord, lest by a multitude
  The new-healed wound of malice should break out,
  Which would be so much the more dangerous

By how much the estate is green and yet ungoverned.
Where every horse bears his commanding rein
And may direct his course as please himself,
As well the fear of harm, as harm apparent,   130
In my opinion, ought to be prevented.

RICHARD

I hope the King made peace with all of us;
And the compact is firm and true in me.

RIVERS

And so in me; and so, I think, in all.
Yet, since it is but green, it should be put
To no apparent likelihood of breach,
Which haply by much company might be urged.
Therefore I say with noble Buckingham
That it is meet so few should fetch the Prince.

HASTINGS

And so say I.   140

RICHARD

Then be it so; and go we to determine
Who they shall be that straight shall post to Ludlow.
Madam, and you, my sister, will you go
To give your censures in this business?

QUEEN ELIZABETH *and* DUCHESS OF YORK

With all our hearts.   *Exeunt*
    Buckingham and Richard remain

BUCKINGHAM

My lord, whoever journeys to the Prince,
For God sake let not us two stay at home;
For by the way I'll sort occasion,
As index to the story we late talked of,
To part the Queen's proud kindred from the Prince.   150

RICHARD

My other self, my counsel's consistory,
My oracle, my prophet, my dear cousin,

I, as a child, will go by thy direction.

Toward Ludlow then, for we'll not stay behind. *Exeunt*

Enter one Citizen at one door, and another at the other

FIRST CITIZEN

Good morrow, neighbour. Whither away so fast?

SECOND CITIZEN

I promise you, I scarcely know myself.

Hear you the news abroad?

FIRST CITIZEN   Yes, that the King is dead.

SECOND CITIZEN

Ill news, by 'r Lady – seldom comes the better.

I fear, I fear 'twill prove a giddy world.

     Enter another Citizen

THIRD CITIZEN

Neighbours, God speed!

FIRST CITIZEN   Give you good morrow, sir.

THIRD CITIZEN

Doth the news hold of good King Edward's death?

SECOND CITIZEN

Ay, sir, it is too true. God help the while!

THIRD CITIZEN

Then, masters, look to see a troublous world.

FIRST CITIZEN

10   No, no! By God's good grace his son shall reign.

THIRD CITIZEN

Woe to that land that's governed by a child!

SECOND CITIZEN

In him there is a hope of government,

Which, in his nonage, council under him,

And, in his full and ripened years, himself,

No doubt shall then, and till then, govern well.

FIRST CITIZEN

    So stood the state when Henry the Sixth
    Was crowned in Paris but at nine months old.

THIRD CITIZEN

    Stood the state so? No, no, good friends, God wot!
    For then this land was famously enriched
    With politic grave counsel; then the King   20
    Had virtuous uncles to protect his grace.

FIRST CITIZEN

    Why, so hath this, both by his father and mother.

THIRD CITIZEN

    Better it were they all came by his father,
    Or by his father there were none at all;
    For emulation who shall now be nearest
    Will touch us all too near, if God prevent not.
    O, full of danger is the Duke of Gloucester,
    And the Queen's sons and brothers haught and proud;
    And were they to be ruled, and not to rule,
    This sickly land might solace as before.   30

FIRST CITIZEN

    Come, come, we fear the worst. All will be well.

THIRD CITIZEN

    When clouds are seen, wise men put on their cloaks;
    When great leaves fall, then winter is at hand;
    When the sun sets, who doth not look for night?
    Untimely storms makes men expect a dearth.
    All may be well; but if God sort it so,
    'Tis more than we deserve or I expect.

SECOND CITIZEN

    Truly, the hearts of men are full of fear;
    You cannot reason almost with a man
    That looks not heavily and full of dread.   40

THIRD CITIZEN

    Before the days of change, still is it so.

II.3–4

> By a divine instinct men's minds mistrust
> Ensuing danger; as by proof we see
> The water swell before a boisterous storm.
> But leave it all to God. Whither away?

SECOND CITIZEN

> Marry, we were sent for to the justices.

THIRD CITIZEN

> And so was I. I'll bear you company.   *Exeunt*

II.4   *Enter Archbishop of York, the young Duke of York,*
                       Queen Elizabeth, and the Duchess of York

ARCHBISHOP

> Last night, I hear, they lay at Stony Stratford,
> And at Northampton they do rest tonight;
> Tomorrow, or next day, they will be here.

DUCHESS OF YORK

> I long with all my heart to see the Prince.
> I hope he is much grown since last I saw him.

QUEEN ELIZABETH

> But I hear no. They say my son of York
> Has almost overta'en him in his growth.

YORK

> Ay, mother; but I would not have it so.

DUCHESS OF YORK

> Why, my young cousin? It is good to grow.

YORK

> Grandam, one night as we did sit at supper,
> My uncle Rivers talked how I did grow
> More than my brother. 'Ay,' quoth my uncle Gloucester,
> 'Small herbs have grace; great weeds do grow apace.'
> And since, methinks, I would not grow so fast,
> Because sweet flowers are slow and weeds make haste.

DUCHESS OF YORK

Good faith, good faith, the saying did not hold
In him that did object the same to thee.
He was the wretched'st thing when he was young,
So long a-growing and so leisurely
That, if his rule were true, he should be gracious.   20

ARCHBISHOP

And so no doubt he is, my gracious madam.

DUCHESS OF YORK

I hope he is; but yet let mothers doubt.

YORK

Now, by my troth, if I had been remembered,
I could have given my uncle's grace a flout
To touch his growth nearer than he touched mine.

DUCHESS OF YORK

How, my young York? I pray thee let me hear it.

YORK

Marry, they say my uncle grew so fast
That he could gnaw a crust at two hours old;
'Twas full two years ere I could get a tooth.
Grandam, this would have been a biting jest.   30

DUCHESS OF YORK

I pray thee, pretty York, who told thee this?

YORK

Grandam, his nurse.

DUCHESS OF YORK

His nurse? Why, she was dead ere thou wast born.

YORK

If 'twere not she, I cannot tell who told me.

QUEEN ELIZABETH

A parlous boy! Go to, you are too shrewd.

DUCHESS OF YORK

Good madam, be not angry with the child.

II.4

QUEEN ELIZABETH
Pitchers have ears.
Enter a Messenger

ARCHBISHOP
Here comes a messenger. What news?

MESSENGER
Such news, my lord, as grieves me to report.

QUEEN ELIZABETH
40 How doth the Prince?

MESSENGER   Well, madam, and in health.

DUCHESS OF YORK
What is thy news?

MESSENGER
Lord Rivers and Lord Grey are sent to Pomfret,
And with them Sir Thomas Vaughan, prisoners.

DUCHESS OF YORK
Who hath committed them?

MESSENGER   The mighty dukes,
Gloucester and Buckingham.

ARCHBISHOP   For what offence?

MESSENGER
The sum of all I can I have disclosed.
Why or for what the nobles were committed
Is all unknown to me, my gracious lord.

QUEEN ELIZABETH
Ay me! I see the ruin of my house.
50 The tiger now hath seized the gentle hind;
Insulting tyranny begins to jut
Upon the innocent and aweless throne.
Welcome destruction, blood, and massacre!
I see, as in a map, the end of all.

DUCHESS OF YORK
Accursèd and unquiet wrangling days,
How many of you have mine eyes beheld!

My husband lost his life to get the crown,
And often up and down my sons were tossed
For me to joy and weep their gain and loss;
And being seated, and domestic broils   60
Clean overblown, themselves the conquerors
Make war upon themselves, brother to brother,
Blood to blood, self against self. O preposterous
And frantic outrage, end thy damnèd spleen,
Or let me die, to look on death no more!

QUEEN ELIZABETH
  Come, come, my boy; we will to sanctuary.
  Madam, farewell.

DUCHESS OF YORK Stay, I will go with you.

QUEEN ELIZABETH
  You have no cause.

ARCHBISHOP (*to the Queen*)
                      My gracious lady, go,
  And thither bear your treasure and your goods.
  For my part, I'll resign unto your grace   70
  The seal I keep; and so betide to me
  As well I tender you and all of yours!
  Go, I'll conduct you to the sanctuary.   *Exeunt*

*

  The trumpets sound. Enter young Prince Edward of III.1
  Wales, the Dukes of Gloucester and Buckingham,
  Lord Cardinal Bourchier, Catesby, with others

BUCKINGHAM
  Welcome, sweet Prince, to London, to your chamber.

RICHARD
  Welcome, dear cousin, my thoughts' sovereign!
  The weary way hath made you melancholy.

PRINCE EDWARD

No, uncle; but our crosses on the way
Have made it tedious, wearisome, and heavy.
I want more uncles here to welcome me.

RICHARD

Sweet Prince, the untainted virtue of your years
Hath not yet dived into the world's deceit;
Nor more can you distinguish of a man
10 Than of his outward show, which, God He knows,
Seldom or never jumpeth with the heart.
Those uncles which you want were dangerous;
Your grace attended to their sugared words
But looked not on the poison of their hearts.
God keep you from them, and from such false friends!

PRINCE EDWARD

God keep me from false friends! – But they were none.

RICHARD

My lord, the Mayor of London comes to greet you.
Enter Lord Mayor and his train

LORD MAYOR

God bless your grace with health and happy days!

PRINCE EDWARD

I thank you, good my lord, and thank you all.
The Lord Mayor and his train stand aside
20 I thought my mother and my brother York
Would long ere this have met us on the way.
Fie, what a slug is Hastings that he comes not
To tell us whether they will come or no!
Enter Lord Hastings

BUCKINGHAM

And, in good time, here comes the sweating lord.

PRINCE EDWARD

Welcome, my lord. What, will our mother come?

HASTINGS

> On what occasion God He knows, not I,
> The Queen your mother and your brother York
> Have taken sanctuary. The tender Prince
> Would fain have come with me to meet your grace,
> But by his mother was perforce withheld.   30

BUCKINGHAM

> Fie, what an indirect and peevish course
> Is this of hers! Lord Cardinal, will your grace
> Persuade the Queen to send the Duke of York
> Unto his princely brother presently?
> If she deny, Lord Hastings, go with him
> And from her jealous arms pluck him perforce.

CARDINAL BOURCHIER

> My Lord of Buckingham, if my weak oratory
> Can from his mother win the Duke of York,
> Anon expect him here; but if she be obdurate
> To mild entreaties, God in heaven forbid   40
> We should infringe the holy privilege
> Of blessed sanctuary! Not for all this land
> Would I be guilty of so deep a sin.

BUCKINGHAM

> You are too senseless-obstinate, my lord,
> Too ceremonious and traditional.
> Weigh it but with the grossness of this age,
> You break not sanctuary in seizing him:
> The benefit thereof is always granted
> To those whose dealings have deserved the place
> And those who have the wit to claim the place.   50
> This prince hath neither claimed it nor deserved it,
> And therefore, in mine opinion, cannot have it.
> Then, taking him from thence that is not there,
> You break no privilege nor charter there.

Oft have I heard of sanctuary men,
But sanctuary children never till now.

CARDINAL BOURCHIER

My lord, you shall overrule my mind for once.
Come on, Lord Hastings, will you go with me?

HASTINGS

I go, my lord.

PRINCE EDWARD

60 Good lords, make all the speedy haste you may.

Exit Cardinal and Hastings

Say, uncle Gloucester, if our brother come,
Where shall we sojourn till our coronation?

RICHARD

Where it seems best unto your royal self.
If I may counsel you, some day or two
Your highness shall repose you at the Tower;
Then where you please, and shall be thought most fit
For your best health and recreation.

PRINCE EDWARD

I do not like the Tower, of any place.
Did Julius Caesar build that place, my lord?

BUCKINGHAM

70 He did, my gracious lord, begin that place,
Which, since, succeeding ages have re-edified.

PRINCE EDWARD

Is it upon record, or else reported
Successively from age to age, he built it?

BUCKINGHAM

Upon record, my gracious lord.

PRINCE EDWARD

But say, my lord, it were not registered,
Methinks the truth should live from age to age,
As 'twere retailed to all posterity,
Even to the general all-ending day.

RICHARD (*aside*)

  So wise so young, they say, do never live long.

PRINCE EDWARD

  What say you, uncle?   80

RICHARD

  I say, without characters fame lives long.

  (*Aside*) Thus, like the formal Vice, Iniquity,

  I moralize two meanings in one word.

PRINCE EDWARD

  That Julius Caesar was a famous man.

  With what his valour did enrich his wit,

  His wit set down to make his valour live.

  Death makes no conquest of this conqueror,

  For now he lives in fame, though not in life.

  I'll tell you what, my cousin Buckingham –

BUCKINGHAM

  What, my gracious lord?   90

PRINCE EDWARD

  An if I live until I be a man,

  I'll win our ancient right in France again

  Or die a soldier as I lived a king.

RICHARD (*aside*)

  Short summers lightly have a forward spring.

     Enter the young Duke of York, Hastings, and
     Cardinal Bourchier

BUCKINGHAM

  Now in good time, here comes the Duke of York.

PRINCE EDWARD

  Richard of York, how fares our loving brother?

YORK

  Well, my dread lord – so must I call you now.

PRINCE EDWARD

  Ay, brother – to our grief, as it is yours.

  Too late he died that might have kept that title,

100   Which by his death hath lost much majesty.

RICHARD

How fares our cousin, noble Lord of York?

YORK

I thank you, gentle uncle. O, my lord,
You said that idle weeds are fast in growth.
The Prince my brother hath outgrown me far.

RICHARD

He hath, my lord.

YORK   And therefore is he idle?

RICHARD

O my fair cousin, I must not say so.

YORK

Then he is more beholding to you than I.

RICHARD

He may command me as my sovereign,
But you have power in me as in a kinsman.

YORK

110   I pray you, uncle, give me this dagger.

RICHARD

My dagger, little cousin? With all my heart.

PRINCE EDWARD

A beggar, brother?

YORK

Of my kind uncle, that I know will give,
And being but a toy, which is no grief to give.

RICHARD

A greater gift than that I'll give my cousin.

YORK

A greater gift? O, that's the sword to it.

RICHARD

Ay, gentle cousin, were it light enough.

YORK

O, then I see you will part but with light gifts!

In weightier things you'll say a beggar nay.

RICHARD

It is too heavy for your grace to wear. 120

YORK

I weigh it lightly, were it heavier.

RICHARD

What, would you have my weapon, little lord?

YORK

I would, that I might thank you as you call me.

RICHARD How?

YORK Little.

PRINCE EDWARD

My Lord of York will still be cross in talk.

Uncle, your grace knows how to bear with him.

YORK

You mean, to bear me, not to bear with me.

Uncle, my brother mocks both you and me.

Because that I am little, like an ape, 130

He thinks that you should bear me on your shoulders.

BUCKINGHAM (*aside to Hastings*)

With what a sharp-provided wit he reasons!

To mitigate the scorn he gives his uncle

He prettily and aptly taunts himself.

So cunning, and so young, is wonderful.

RICHARD

My lord, will't please you pass along?

Myself and my good cousin Buckingham

Will to your mother, to entreat of her

To meet you at the Tower and welcome you.

YORK

What, will you go unto the Tower, my lord? 140

PRINCE EDWARD

My Lord Protector needs will have it so.

III.1

YORK
> I shall not sleep in quiet at the Tower.

RICHARD
> Why, what should you fear?

YORK
> Marry, my uncle Clarence' angry ghost –
> My grandam told me he was murdered there.

PRINCE EDWARD
> I fear no uncles dead.

RICHARD
> Nor none that live, I hope.

PRINCE EDWARD
> An if they live, I hope I need not fear.
> But come, my lord; and with a heavy heart,
150 Thinking on them, go I unto the Tower.
> > *A sennet. Exeunt Prince Edward, York, Hastings,*
> > > *Cardinal Bourchier, and others*
> > *Richard, Buckingham, and Catesby remain*

BUCKINGHAM
> Think you, my lord, this little prating York
> Was not incensèd by his subtle mother
> To taunt and scorn you thus opprobriously?

RICHARD
> No doubt, no doubt. O, 'tis a parlous boy,
> Bold, quick, ingenious, forward, capable.
> He is all the mother's, from the top to toe.

BUCKINGHAM
> Well, let them rest. Come hither, Catesby. Thou art sworn
> As deeply to effect what we intend
> As closely to conceal what we impart.
160 Thou know'st our reasons urged upon the way.
> What think'st thou? Is it not an easy matter
> To make William Lord Hastings of our mind
> For the instalment of this noble Duke

In the seat royal of this famous isle?

CATESBY

He for his father's sake so loves the Prince
That he will not be won to aught against him.

BUCKINGHAM

What think'st thou then of Stanley? Will not he?

CATESBY

He will do all in all as Hastings doth.

BUCKINGHAM

Well then, no more but this: go, gentle Catesby,
And, as it were afar off, sound thou Lord Hastings   170
How he doth stand affected to our purpose,
And summon him tomorrow to the Tower
To sit about the coronation.
If thou dost find him tractable to us,
Encourage him, and tell him all our reasons;
If he be leaden, icy, cold, unwilling,
Be thou so too, and so break off the talk,
And give us notice of his inclination;
For we tomorrow hold divided councils,
Wherein thyself shalt highly be employed.   180

RICHARD

Commend me to Lord William. Tell him, Catesby,
His ancient knot of dangerous adversaries
Tomorrow are let blood at Pomfret Castle,
And bid my lord, for joy of this good news,
Give Mistress Shore one gentle kiss the more.

BUCKINGHAM

Good Catesby, go, effect this business soundly.

CATESBY

My good lords both, with all the heed I can.

RICHARD

Shall we hear from you, Catesby, ere we sleep?

CATESBY
  You shall, my lord.

RICHARD

190 At Crosby House, there shall you find us both.

                                        Exit Catesby

BUCKINGHAM
  Now, my lord, what shall we do if we perceive
  Lord Hastings will not yield to our complots?

RICHARD
  Chop off his head! Something we will determine.
  And look when I am King, claim thou of me
  The earldom of Hereford and all the movables
  Whereof the King my brother was possessed.

BUCKINGHAM
  I'll claim that promise at your grace's hand.

RICHARD
  And look to have it yielded with all kindness.
  Come, let us sup betimes, that afterwards

200 We may digest our complots in some form.   *Exeunt*

III.2   *Enter a Messenger to the door of Hastings*

MESSENGER My lord! My lord!

HASTINGS (*within*) Who knocks?

MESSENGER One from the Lord Stanley.

           Enter Lord Hastings

HASTINGS What is't a clock?

MESSENGER Upon the stroke of four.

HASTINGS
  Cannot my Lord Stanley sleep these tedious nights?

MESSENGER
  So it appears by that I have to say:
  First, he commends him to your noble self.

HASTINGS

    What then?

MESSENGER

    Then certifies your lordship that this night   10
    He dreamt the boar had razèd off his helm.
    Besides, he says there are two councils kept;
    And that may be determined at the one
    Which may make you and him to rue at th'other.
    Therefore he sends to know your lordship's pleasure,
    If you will presently take horse with him
    And with all speed post with him toward the north
    To shun the danger that his soul divines.

HASTINGS

    Go, fellow, go, return unto thy lord;
    Bid him not fear the separated council.   20
    His honour and myself are at the one,
    And at the other is my good friend Catesby;
    Where nothing can proceed that toucheth us
    Whereof I shall not have intelligence.
    Tell him his fears are shallow, without instance;
    And for his dreams, I wonder he's so simple
    To trust the mockery of unquiet slumbers.
    To fly the boar before the boar pursues
    Were to incense the boar to follow us,
    And make pursuit where he did mean no chase.   30
    Go, bid thy master rise and come to me,
    And we will both together to the Tower,
    Where he shall see the boar will use us kindly.

MESSENGER

    I'll go, my lord, and tell him what you say.   *Exit*
      Enter Catesby

CATESBY

    Many good morrows to my noble lord!

III.2

HASTINGS

Good morrow, Catesby; you are early stirring.
What news, what news, in this our tottering state?

CATESBY

It is a reeling world indeed, my lord,
And I believe will never stand upright
40 Till Richard wear the garland of the realm.

HASTINGS

How! Wear the garland! Dost thou mean the
        crown?

CATESBY

Ay, my good lord.

HASTINGS

I'll have this crown of mine cut from my shoulders
Before I'll see the crown so foul misplaced.
But canst thou guess that he doth aim at it?

CATESBY

Ay, on my life, and hopes to find you forward
Upon his party for the gain thereof;
And thereupon he sends you this good news,
That this same very day your enemies,
50 The kindred of the Queen, must die at Pomfret.

HASTINGS

Indeed I am no mourner for that news,
Because they have been still my adversaries;
But that I'll give my voice on Richard's side
To bar my master's heirs in true descent –
God knows I will not do it, to the death!

CATESBY

God keep your lordship in that gracious mind!

HASTINGS

But I shall laugh at this a twelvemonth hence,
That they which brought me in my master's hate,
I live to look upon their tragedy.

Well, Catesby, ere a fortnight make me older,   60
I'll send some packing that yet think not on't.

CATESBY

'Tis a vile thing to die, my gracious lord,
When men are unprepared and look not for it.

HASTINGS

O monstrous, monstrous! And so falls it out
With Rivers, Vaughan, Grey; and so 'twill do
With some men else, that think themselves as safe
As thou and I, who as thou know'st are dear
To princely Richard and to Buckingham.

CATESBY

The princes both make high account of you –
(*Aside*) For they account his head upon the Bridge.   70

HASTINGS

I know they do, and I have well deserved it.
        Enter Earl of Derby
Come on, come on! Where is your boar-spear, man?
Fear you the boar, and go so unprovided?

DERBY

My lord, good morrow. Good morrow, Catesby.
You may jest on, but, by the Holy Rood,
I do not like these several councils, I.

HASTINGS

My lord, I hold my life as dear as you do yours,
And never in my days, I do protest,
Was it so precious to me as 'tis now.
Think you, but that I know our state secure,   80
I would be so triumphant as I am?

DERBY

The lords at Pomfret, when they rode from London,
Were jocund and supposed their states were sure,
And they indeed had no cause to mistrust;
But yet you see how soon the day o'ercast.

This sudden stab of rancour I misdoubt.
Pray God, I say, I prove a needless coward!
What, shall we toward the Tower? The day is spent.

HASTINGS
Come, come, have with you. Wot you what, my lord?
90 Today the lords you talked of are beheaded.

DERBY
They, for their truth, might better wear their heads
Than some that have accused them wear their hats.
But come, my lord, let us away.

Enter a Pursuivant also named Hastings

HASTINGS
Go on before. I'll talk with this good fellow.

Exeunt Earl of Derby and Catesby

How now, Hastings! How goes the world with thee?

PURSUIVANT
The better that your lordship please to ask.

HASTINGS
I tell thee, man, 'tis better with me now
Than when I met thee last where now we meet.
Then was I going prisoner to the Tower
100 By the suggestion of the Queen's allies;
But now I tell thee – keep it to thyself –
This day those enemies are put to death,
And I in better state than e'er I was.

PURSUIVANT
God hold it, to your honour's good content!

HASTINGS
Gramercy, Hastings. There, drink that for me.

Throws him his purse

PURSUIVANT
I thank your honour.   *Exit Pursuivant*

Enter a Priest

PRIEST

  Well met, my lord. I am glad to see your honour.

HASTINGS

  I thank thee, good Sir John, with all my heart.

  I am in your debt for your last exercise;

  Come the next Sabbath, and I will content you.   110

     He whispers in his ear

PRIEST

  I'll wait upon your lordship.

     Enter Buckingham

BUCKINGHAM

  What, talking with a priest, Lord Chamberlain?

  Your friends at Pomfret, they do need the priest;

  Your honour hath no shriving work in hand.

HASTINGS

  Good faith, and when I met this holy man,

  The men you talk of came into my mind.

  What, go you toward the Tower?

BUCKINGHAM

  I do, my lord, but long I cannot stay there.

  I shall return before your lordship thence.

HASTINGS

  Nay, like enough, for I stay dinner there.   120

BUCKINGHAM (*aside*)

  And supper too, although thou know'st it not.

  – Come, will you go?

HASTINGS   I'll wait upon your lordship.

     Exeunt

III.3 *Enter Sir Richard Ratcliffe, with halberds, carrying*
Rivers, Grey, and Vaughan to death at Pomfret

RIVERS

    Sir Richard Ratcliffe, let me tell thee this:
    Today shalt thou behold a subject die
    For truth, for duty, and for loyalty.

GREY

    God bless the Prince from all the pack of you!
    A knot you are of damnèd bloodsuckers.

VAUGHAN

    You live that shall cry woe for this hereafter.

RATCLIFFE

    Dispatch! The limit of your lives is out.

RIVERS

    O Pomfret, Pomfret! O thou bloody prison,
    Fatal and ominous to noble peers!
10   Within the guilty closure of thy walls
    Richard the Second here was hacked to death;
    And, for more slander to thy dismal seat,
    We give to thee our guiltless blood to drink.

GREY

    Now Margaret's curse is fallen upon our heads,
    When she exclaimed on Hastings, you, and I,
    For standing by when Richard stabbed her son.

RIVERS

    Then cursed she Richard, then cursed she Buckingham,
    Then cursed she Hastings. O, remember, God,
    To hear her prayer for them, as now for us!
20   And for my sister and her princely sons,
    Be satisfied, dear God, with our true blood,
    Which, as Thou know'st, unjustly must be spilt.

RATCLIFFE

    Make haste. The hour of death is expiate.

RIVERS

  Come, Grey; come, Vaughan; let us here embrace.
  Farewell, until we meet again in heaven.   *Exeunt*

    Enter Buckingham, Derby, Hastings, Bishop of Ely,   III.4
    Norfolk, Ratcliffe, Lovel, with others, at a table

HASTINGS

  Now, noble peers, the cause why we are met
  Is to determine of the coronation.
  In God's name, speak. When is the royal day?

BUCKINGHAM

  Is all things ready for the royal time?

DERBY

  It is, and wants but nomination.

BISHOP OF ELY

  Tomorrow then I judge a happy day.

BUCKINGHAM

  Who knows the Lord Protector's mind herein?
  Who is most inward with the noble Duke?

BISHOP OF ELY

  Your grace, we think, should soonest know his mind.

BUCKINGHAM

  We know each other's faces; for our hearts,   10
  He knows no more of mine than I of yours;
  Or I of his, my lord, than you of mine.
  Lord Hastings, you and he are near in love.

HASTINGS

  I thank his grace, I know he loves me well;
  But, for his purpose in the coronation,
  I have not sounded him, nor he delivered
  His gracious pleasure any way therein;
  But you, my honourable lords, may name the time,

And in the Duke's behalf I'll give my voice,

20 Which, I presume, he'll take in gentle part.

Enter Richard, Duke of Gloucester

BISHOP OF ELY

In happy time, here comes the Duke himself.

RICHARD

My noble lords and cousins all, good morrow.
I have been long a sleeper; but I trust
My absence doth neglect no great design
Which by my presence might have been concluded.

BUCKINGHAM

Had you not come upon your cue, my lord,
William Lord Hastings had pronounced your part –
I mean, your voice for crowning of the King.

RICHARD

Than my Lord Hastings no man might be bolder.

30 His lordship knows me well, and loves me well.
My Lord of Ely, when I was last in Holborn
I saw good strawberries in your garden there.
I do beseech you send for some of them.

BISHOP OF ELY

Marry and will, my lord, with all my heart.

Exit Bishop

RICHARD

Cousin of Buckingham, a word with you.

Takes him aside

Catesby hath sounded Hastings in our business
And finds the testy gentleman so hot
That he will lose his head ere give consent
His master's child, as worshipfully he terms it,

40 Shall lose the royalty of England's throne.

BUCKINGHAM

Withdraw yourself awhile. I'll go with you.

Exeunt Richard and Buckingham

DERBY

    We have not yet set down this day of triumph.
    Tomorrow, in my judgement, is too sudden;
    For I myself am not so well provided
    As else I would be, were the day prolonged.
       Enter the Bishop of Ely

BISHOP OF ELY

    Where is my lord the Duke of Gloucester?
    I have sent for these strawberries.

HASTINGS

    His grace looks cheerfully and smooth this morning;
    There's some conceit or other likes him well
    When that he bids good morrow with such spirit.   50
    I think there's never a man in Christendom
    Can lesser hide his love or hate than he,
    For by his face straight shall you know his heart.

DERBY

    What of his heart perceive you in his face
    By any livelihood he showed today?

HASTINGS

    Marry, that with no man here he is offended;
    For were he, he had shown it in his looks.

DERBY

    I pray God he be not, I say.
       Enter Richard and Buckingham

RICHARD

    I pray you all, tell me what they deserve
    That do conspire my death with devilish plots   60
    Of damnèd witchcraft, and that have prevailed
    Upon my body with their hellish charms.

HASTINGS

    The tender love I bear your grace, my lord,
    Makes me most forward in this princely presence
    To doom th'offenders: whatsoever they be,

I say, my lord, they have deservèd death.

RICHARD

Then be your eyes the witness of their evil.
See how I am bewitched: behold, mine arm
Is like a blasted sapling, withered up;
70 And this is Edward's wife, that monstrous witch,
Consorted with that harlot, strumpet Shore,
That by their witchcraft thus have markèd me.

HASTINGS

If they have done this deed, my noble lord –

RICHARD

If? Thou protector of this damnèd strumpet,
Talk'st thou to me of ifs? Thou art a traitor.
Off with his head! Now by Saint Paul I swear
I will not dine until I see the same!
Lovel and Ratcliffe, look that it be done.
The rest that love me, rise and follow me.   *Exeunt*
       Lovel and Ratcliffe remain, with Lord Hastings

HASTINGS

80 Woe, woe for England, not a whit for me!
For I, too fond, might have prevented this.
Stanley did dream the boar did raze our helms,
And I did scorn it and disdain to fly.
Three times today my footcloth horse did stumble,
And started when he looked upon the Tower,
As loath to bear me to the slaughterhouse.
O, now I need the priest that spake to me!
I now repent I told the pursuivant,
As too triumphing, how mine enemies
90 Today at Pomfret bloodily were butchered,
And I myself secure, in grace and favour.
O Margaret, Margaret, now thy heavy curse
Is lighted on poor Hastings' wretched head!

RATCLIFFE

Come, come, dispatch! The Duke would be at dinner.
Make a short shrift; he longs to see your head.

HASTINGS

O momentary grace of mortal men,
Which we more hunt for than the grace of God!
Who builds his hope in air of your good looks
Lives like a drunken sailor on a mast,
Ready with every nod to tumble down   100
Into the fatal bowels of the deep.

LOVEL

Come, come, dispatch! 'Tis bootless to exclaim.

HASTINGS

O bloody Richard! Miserable England!
I prophesy the fearfull'st time to thee
That ever wretched age hath looked upon.
Come, lead me to the block; bear him my head.
They smile at me who shortly shall be dead.   *Exeunt*

Enter Richard, Duke of Gloucester, and Buckingham,   III.5
in rotten armour, marvellous ill-favoured

RICHARD

Come, cousin, canst thou quake and change thy colour,
Murder thy breath in middle of a word,
And then again begin, and stop again,
As if thou wert distraught and mad with terror?

BUCKINGHAM

Tut, I can counterfeit the deep tragedian,
Speak and look back, and pry on every side,
Tremble and start at wagging of a straw;
Intending deep suspicion, ghastly looks
Are at my service, like enforcèd smiles;

10 And both are ready in their offices,
At any time to grace my stratagems.
But what, is Catesby gone?

RICHARD

He is; and see, he brings the Mayor along.
Enter the Lord Mayor and Catesby

BUCKINGHAM Lord Mayor –

RICHARD Look to the drawbridge there!

BUCKINGHAM Hark! A drum.

RICHARD Catesby, o'erlook the walls.

BUCKINGHAM Lord Mayor, the reason we have sent –

RICHARD

Look back! Defend thee! Here are enemies!

BUCKINGHAM

20 God and our innocence defend and guard us!
Enter Lovel and Ratcliffe, with Hastings' head

RICHARD

Be patient, they are friends, Ratcliffe and Lovel.

LOVEL

Here is the head of that ignoble traitor,
The dangerous and unsuspected Hastings.

RICHARD

So dear I loved the man that I must weep.
I took him for the plainest harmless creature
That breathed upon the earth a Christian;
Made him my book, wherein my soul recorded
The history of all her secret thoughts.
So smooth he daubed his vice with show of virtue

30 That, his apparent open guilt omitted –
I mean, his conversation with Shore's wife –
He lived from all attainder of suspects.

BUCKINGHAM

Well, well, he was the covert'st sheltered traitor.
Would you imagine, or almost believe,